*W*HEN one is being bought and sold like an animal," Jared said grimly, "hatred is the only thing which keeps at bay the humiliation and the despair. Seeing you reminded me of all that life could never be again and at that moment, Miss Court, I hated you more than any living being." Then his expression relaxed a little, and a faint smile touched his lips. "Even though you were the fairest sight I had seen for many weary months."

The color in her cheeks deepened to scarlet, and she said angrily, "That is enough! You forget yourself!"

"Yes!" Jared's face was suddenly white, his voice bitter. "For a moment I did forget. My apologies, Miss Court."

For the rest of the way, Jared's manner was rigidly correct. He betrayed no emotion of any kind. Bethany was angry and distressed, and in some curious way felt that it was she who was in the wrong....

No More A-Roving

a novel by

SYLVIA THORPE

FAWCETT CREST • NEW YORK

NO MORE A-ROVING

THIS BOOK CONTAINS THE COMPLETE TEXT OF
THE ORIGINAL HARDCOVER EDITION.

Published by Fawcett Crest Books, a unit of CBS Publica-
tions, the Consumer Publishing Division of CBS Inc.,
by arrangement with the Hutchinson Publishing Group.

Copyright © 1970 by Sylvia Thorpe

ALL RIGHTS RESERVED

ISBN: 0-449-24080-0

Printed in the United States of America

10 9 8 7 6 5 4 3 2 1

No More
A-Roving

One

The ship called the *Happy Return* had come safely to the end of her voyage across the Atlantic. With her sails white against the blue-green water, and the British flag trailing from her mast-head, she had glided past the guardian fort and into Bridgetown harbor, where she now rode peacefully at anchor. Yet her beauty under sail, and the serenity of her as she lay at her anchorage, were made a mockery of by the misery of her wretched cargo—nearly a hundred rebels-convict, condemned to ten years' servitude in the plantations for their part in the Duke of Monmouth's recent, ill-fated uprising.

"The *Happy Return*!" Bethany Court said bitterly when she heard of it. "A ship bringing men into slavery which few of them will survive. Merciful Heaven, what cruel irony!"

There were few in Barbados who shared Bethany's angry concern, or saw anything wrong in purchasing their fellow-countrymen as slaves. Criminals must be punished, and these men, farmers and artisans until they took up arms against their lawful King, would be a valuable addition to the skilled workers of the colony. Even Bethany's own father, Matthew Court, was eager to secure some of them.

So eager was he that when the rebels-convict were brought ashore, he was the first of the local planters to arrive on the scene. Bethany was with him. Finding it impossible to turn him from his purpose, she had resolved to make use of it, if she could, to aid her unceasing efforts on behalf of the slaves for whom she alone, it seemed, felt any compassion.

The convicts had been assembled in an open, cobbled space near the waterfront, guarded by a detachment of the Barbados Militia, and Bethany and her father arrived just as the last batch to be brought ashore was being herded to join the rest. The young officer commanding the militia was acquainted with the Court family and hurried to greet them, delighted to have the tedium of his present duty enlivened by the unexpected presence of the prettiest girl in Bridgetown.

"My dear Miss Court, this is an unlooked-for pleasure," he exclaimed, "though I guessed that your father would be among the first to look over this sorry crowd of rascals. Permit me to advise you to keep your distance from them, and preferably not to windward. They are by no means fragrant."

She made some civil reply, then, as he turned to greet her father, began to study the rebels-convict. There was some justification for Captain Maynard's callous warning, for the prisoners were in a wretched condition, ragged and filthy, with matted hair and beards. Many bore the fresh scars of wounds sustained during the brief rebellion, others were obviously ailing, and all appeared to be sunk in the apathy of utter despair. Some of them had dropped down to sit huddled on the dusty cobbles, the rest stood with slumped shoulders and bowed heads, apparently numbed by suffering already endured, and the prospect of that which lay ahead.

Only one of them seemed to have retained any spark of defiance, and as Bethany's compassionate gaze passed over the uneven ranks, she was struck by the sharp contrast between this man and his companions. Tall, and made to appear even more so by the arrogant set of his shoulders, he stood with head erect, looking scornfully about him at the red-coated militia and the crowd of staring idlers. Bethany, remembering her father saying that only the rank and file of the rebel army had been transported, regarded him with a puzzled frown. He did not look like a man of humble stock, for though his clothing was so dirty and ragged that it was impossible to judge what it had once been, and his lank, dark hair fell about his face to mingle with an equally unkempt beard, there was that in his bearing which set him apart from the rest of the prisoners.

He was standing only a little way from where she sat her horse in the shade cast by a nearby building, and as she watched him, he turned his head and looked straight at her. He had eyes of a light, cold gray, striking by contrast to the darkness of hair and brow, and the hostility and contempt in them struck her like a blow. The hard glance flicked over her, from her broad, plumed hat to the hem of her dark blue riding-habit, returned for an instant to her face, and then passed indifferently on, leaving her oddly disturbed. Resentment, even hatred, from a man in his situation was understandable, but there seemed no reason for that look of unutterable contempt.

Because she was still looking in his direction, she noticed the man beside him, and pity once again took command of her, for here the fierce sunlight was beating down on stooped shoulders and silvery hair. He looked so frail and old it seemed remarkable that

he should still be on his feet, and even as Bethany
watched, he reeled suddenly against the tall man at
his side. At once the other turned in quick concern, to
clasp his arm and lower him gently to the ground,
saying something obviously intended to convey
encouragement and reassurance. The action was so
much at variance with his former haughty bearing
that Bethany's curiosity was even further aroused.

She had little time to speculate upon it, for at that
moment a horse was reined in alongside her own, and
its rider exclaimed in an angry, astonished tone:

"Bethany! What in the fiend's name are you doing
here?"

It was the voice of Pierce Warren, to whom she was
betrothed. She turned to look at him, saying, with a
tranquillity belied by the spark of answering annoyance in her blue eyes:

"Nothing, Pierce, which makes it necessary for
you to use that tone. I came with Father."

"I should hope so, indeed!" he replied shortly.
"Even you would hardly be rash enough to come
alone. What I cannot understand is why you should
wish to come at all—or why your father allowed it."

Captain Maynard moved discreetly away, for a
quarrel was clearly brewing and he had no wish to be
a witness of it. Mr. Court had already dismounted
and was walking along the straggling lines of
prisoners, deep in conversation with one of the local
agents for labor supply. His head overseer, Will
Hopson, who accompanied him, was following, and
from time to time Mr. Court would single out one of
the convicts, there would be a brief discussion with
the agent, and then the man thus chosen was put into
the overseer's charge. Pierce watched the proceed-
ings moodily for a moment or two and then turned
again to Bethany.

"Let me take you home. This is no place for you."

She had not replied to his previous remark, and the

set of her lips should have warned him that he was treading on dangerous ground. She said quietly:

"I shall wait for Father. Since he sees no harm in my coming here, it is not for you to do so, and if I can find it in my power to ease the lot of even one of these unfortunate men, I shall consider the time well spent."

"Unfortunate!" he repeated scornfully. "A pack of confounded rebels! They should count themselves lucky that their lives have been spared; for it is a mercy they have done nothing to deserve."

"What mercy lies in sparing a man's life in order to sell him into slavery like some brute beast?" she demanded hotly. "Besides, Father says that profit, and not mercy, is the purpose behind such sentences. A dead rebel is worth nothing. A live one will fetch ten or fifteen pounds here, or in Jamaica. Oh, it sickens me to think of it!"

"With respect, Bethany, your father has of late talked too freely to you upon subjects beyond your understanding. Such matters are not a woman's concern."

"They should be everyone's concern," she retorted. "At least Father accepts that a woman may have some thoughts in her head beyond keeping a man's house and bearing his children. If that is all you seek in a wife, Pierce, you would do better to marry Esther."

"There is no need to jeer at your sister because you are in an ill humor with me," he said stiffly. "No doubt when the time comes for Esther to marry, she will prove a good and dutiful wife."

"No doubt!" There was still an edge to Bethany's voice. "Esther is a model of meekness and obedience, and what more could any man ask? But *I* shall never be content to become merely your echo, Pierce! You had better face that fact before it is too late."

He looked at her with an exasperation faintly

tinged with misgiving. Their marriage had been agreed upon by their respective fathers years before, and from a practical point of view was an excellent match. Pierce was heir to his father's flourishing plantation, and, since Matthew Court had no son, the prosperous estate of Courtlands would be divided between his twin daughters, Bethany and Esther. The marriage would make Pierce one of the richest men in the colony, and he would have been prepared to marry Bethany even if she had been stupid and plain. He could count himself doubly fortunate that she was neither, and if her quick temper and independence of thought and action caused him an occasional qualm, he stifled it with the reflection that matters would be very different once they were married.

His expression softened a little as he looked at her. Clear-cut profile beneath the sweep of the hat's broad brim; golden hair elaborately curled in the fashion of the day; slender, rounded figure emphasized by the stylish riding-habit of heavy silk. A first impression of Bethany Court was of golden prettiness verging upon real beauty, but a perceptive eye was needed to observe that there was also considerable strength of character in that enchanting face. Pierce lacked such perception, but the sight of Bethany never failed to stir him; the childhood playmate had become a woman infinitely desirable, and he was filled with jealous pride by the thought that she was soon to be his wife.

"I would not have you change, Bethany," he said recklessly, and at that moment sincerely believed that he meant it. "Nor is it right that we should quarrel over a crowd of miserable slaves. Come, say that you forgive me, and let us cry truce to the whole sorry affair."

She turned at once towards him, smiling and putting out her hand, for her temper, always quick to rise, was as prompt to cool again. He took her gloved fingers and lifted them to his lips, and Captain Maynard, unobtrusively watching from a little distance, concluded that peace had been restored.

By this time, other planters had arrived, and the crowd of rebels-convict was rapidly being divided into smaller groups. Mr. Court's overseer now had a number in his charge, Pierce's father had secured some half-dozen, and as the other landowners made their purchases the number remaining dwindled steadily. Pierce again tried, more diplomatically, to persuade Bethany to leave, but she insisted on waiting until her father joined them. This he eventually did, and as soon as he had greeted Pierce, she said urgently:

"Father, that old man yonder. Pray take him also."

Mr. Court and Pierce followed the direction of her pointing hand. The old man she had noticed earlier still huddled on the cobblestones, alone now, for all those about him had gone. Mr. Court frowned, and Pierce said bluntly:

"It will be money wasted, sir. I doubt he will survive as much as a month."

"All the more reason to do what we can for him," Bethany broke in. "Oh, Father, please! And there is a boy over there who I'll swear is not more than sixteen, and ailing, too. We can find light work for them."

Mr. Court turned and beckoned to the agent. Privately he shared Pierce's opinion, but he was seldom able to refuse Bethany when she pleaded for anything. In a short space of time the transaction was concluded, and the old man and the skinny, frightened lad sent to join the group in Hopson's charge. The overseer was to march the newly acquired slaves the short distance to Courtlands, and as he herded them away Bethany caught a glimpse among them of an arrogantly poised dark head.

There, she reflected wryly, was one man at least who
would neither look for favors, nor be grateful for
them.

"Do you not think, Bethany," Esther suggested
diffidently, "that you ought to show less concern for
the slaves? Pierce does not approve, you know."

Diffidence came naturally to Esther. She was
completely different from Bethany, a small, timid
girl with light brown hair, eyes of indeterminate
blue-gray, and a soft, breathless voice. Pretty enough
in a nondescript way, yet so completely overshad-
owed by her striking twin that she was invariably
referred to as "Bethany Court's sister," while her
self-effacing, almost apologetic manner irritated
many people, including her father and, at times,
Bethany herself. This was one of those occasions.

"Then Pierce must learn to approve," Bethany
said crisply, "or, at least, to accept it. I do no more
than common humanity demands."

"It will be different when you are married. Mr.
Warren will not permit you to interfere in the
management of Warrenfield as Father allows you to
do here, and it will not matter whether Pierce
approves, or not."

Bethany frowned, recognizing the truth of this.
Pierce's father, like most planters, looked on his
slaves as mere beasts of burden, to be worked to their
uttermost capacity, given no better food and shelter
than was necessary to keep them alive, and hunted
down without mercy if they tried to escape. It was no
wonder, she thought with her usual helpless anger,
that a slave uprising was a constant and dreaded
possibility, so that the big plantation houses had to
be fortified like castles in order to provide a safe
refuge if it occurred, while the slightest hint of
rebellion was punished with appalling brutality.

"I shall do what I can," she said after a moment, "and try to win Pierce to my way of thinking. Warrenfield will be his one day."

"You will not convince him." Esther warned her timidly. "Oh, do not let concern for a few wretched slaves come between you! They are not worth it. The blacks are savages, and the white slaves criminals who are being justly punished."

"They are all human souls, Esther, no matter what color their skin, or what crimes they have committed. It is not right that their fellow men should buy and sell them like cattle. That is what our mother believed, and tried to teach us to believe also."

"Mother came from England, and never accustomed herself to the ways of the New World. *You* know that without slaves, the plantations could not be worked. Bethany, I beg of you, do not persist in this attitude after you are married. It will not be fair to Pierce. He will be torn between his fondness for you, and duty to his father, and it is he who will suffer."

She broke off, for Bethany was no longer listening. They were riding home through the plantation, along one of the avenues which intersected the great blocks of sugar-cane, where armed overseers kept constant watch on the Negro slaves working in the fields. Now, at a junction of two such avenues, Bethany had drawn rein to stare at a group of blacks a short distance away. There was one white man among them.

"That is strange," she said with a frown. "I thought the white servants were to be employed at the sugar-mill, or practicing their own trades, not as gang labor in the fields."

She wheeled her horse and rode towards the little group, Esther following with a sigh of exasperation. As they drew closer to the slaves, they saw that the head overseer was approaching from the opposite direction.

He and Bethany reached the slaves at the same time, and after a curt nod in answer to his respectful greeting, she said sharply, indicating the white man: "What is the reason for this? My father does not want skilled laborers wasted upon field work."

Hopson looked up at her with a gleam of resentment in his eyes, though his manner lost none of the respect due to the daughter of his employer. He was a big man with heavy, sullen features, and, like the other overseers, carried a pistol at his belt and a coiled whip in his hand.

"By your leave, Miss Court, this man is not a skilled laborer and has naught to recommend him save a strong back. Besides, he is a mutinous dog, best employed out here in the fields where he cannot stir up trouble."

Bethany looked again at the object of their argument. He had paused in his task of digging an irrigation channel and now stood leaning on his shovel, watching her. She had no difficulty in recognizing him, for those hostile, light gray eyes were not easily forgotten.

She beckoned to him to come nearer, and after an instant's hesitation, while he seemed to be debating whether or not to obey, he moved forward until he stood midway between her and Hopson. Bethany studied him curiously. Like the other slaves, he was barefoot and clad only in breeches of rough homespun, his face disfigured by the matted beard, yet for all his unkempt appearance there was still some quality about him which made him seem different from any other bond-servant she had ever seen.

"What is your name?" she asked, and felt no surprise when he answered her in the voice of an educated man.

"It is Vernon, madam. Jared Vernon." He looked up at her, and once again she saw contempt and derision blazing in his eyes. He bowed, with a courtly grace as mocking as the words which accompanied it. "Your most humble servant."

Hopson's hand moved with practiced speed, and the lash of his whip coiled with a sound like a pistol shot across the slave's naked shoulders. Jared Vernon spun round to face him, the heavy shovel raised and such fury in his face that the overseer fell back a pace and dropped a hand to the pistol at his belt, for he had seen slaves goaded to madness before. Esther cried out, and her horse, already startled by the swift movements and the crack of the whip so close at hand, shied violently.

Esther, no horsewoman, screamed again, and Vernon, dropping his makeshift weapon, sprang to seize the horse's bridle. After a brief struggle he succeeded in mastering the frightened animal; it stood quiet again, trembling, while he fondled it and spoke quiet, reassuring words.

The whole thing had happened so quickly that the Negro groom in attendance on the sisters had not had time to come to his mistress's aid, while Hopson still stood with one hand on the pistol-butt and his whip trailing from the other. Esther was sobbing with shock, but Bethany, soothing her own nervous mount, remained composed even though she was rather pale.

"We have reason to be grateful to you, Mr. Vernon," she said, and never even paused to wonder why she should address this convict-slave as an equal. "I will speak to my father. Be patient a little, and I promise that you shall be found more fitting work than this."

She signed to the groom to lead Esther's horse, since Esther herself was for the moment incapable of handling it, and they moved away. Jared Vernon stood staring after them with a puzzled frown, until a savage command from the overseer recalled his attention. Then he picked up the shovel, and with an almost imperceptible shrug returned to his lowly labors.

When they reached the house, Bethany left Esther in the care of Tabitha, the old mulatto woman who had been their nurse when they were children, and went to look for her father. Finding him in the room where he transacted the business of the plantation, she hurriedly described what had happened, and concluded by saying urgently:

"Father, he has the speech and manner of a gentleman. You cannot condemn him to labor in the fields like a Negro."

Mr. Court was frowning. "I remember the man. A lean, vigorous fellow, well fitted to hard work in this climate—that is why I bought him. Yet if he is a gentleman, how comes he here? Monmouth's captured officers, and others important in the rebellion, were put to death."

"Why not question him, sir?" she suggested. "It seems absurd to waste a man of education on common field work. Besides, these rebels-convict are not really criminals, are they?"

"King James and his Ministers would not agree with you," Mr. Court replied dryly, "though it is true that most of the rebels are honest men, guilty of little but folly, and hatred of the Catholic faith."

He was silent for a moment, frowning at the thoughts his own words had evoked. Matthew Court was no supporter of the pretensions of the bastard Duke of Monmouth, but a lifetime in the Indies had made him too familiar with the atrocities committed, in the name of religion, by Catholic Spain, for him to feel anything but misgiving now that there was a Catholic monarch on the English throne. His loyalty to the Crown was tempered by a certain sympathy with those who, however misguided their choice of a leader, had sought to re-establish the Protestant faith, and the news which Bethany had just brought him was disquieting.

"Gentleman or no, the man is still a convicted rebel," he said at length, "and Hopson, you tell me, says that he is mutinous."

"Will Hopson would say anything to justify disregarding your commands," she retorted scornfully. "Please, Father, question Jared Vernon! We owe him that much, at least, for what he did today. If Esther's horse had bolted..."

"How like your mother you are," Mr. Court broke in quietly. "Thus would she plead the cause of anyone whom she believed unjustly used. Very well, I will send for the man."

He summoned one of the house-slaves and gave orders for a message to be sent to the overseer. When they were alone again, Bethany said hopefully:

"May I stay, Father? I promise not to say a word while you question Vernon, but I own that I am curious to hear what he has to say."

He gave his permission. It was freely said in Bridgetown that Matthew Court could deny Bethany nothing, and those who could remember his late wife had no doubt why. In looks and character Bethany was exactly like her mother, as Mrs. Court had been when she first came to Barbados, an adored and adoring bride whom Matthew Court had met and married during a brief visit to England. Mrs. Court had never been strong, and after the birth of her twin daughters her health steadily worsened; she died when the girls were fourteen, and from that time Bethany had been mistress of her father's house. He paid almost as much heed to her wishes as he had done to his wife's, so that friends and neighbors prophesied that no good would come of it, and wondered what would happen when the girl married.

If such doubts troubled Mr. Court, he did not

betray them. He was a reserved man, of deep
emotions not easily expressed, and his great love for
and pride in the first-born of his twin daughters
showed itself only in the confidence he reposed in her,
and in the way he heeded her opinions on such
matters as the treatment of the slaves.

While they waited for Jared Vernon, Mr. Court
resumed his study of some documents, which Bethany's arrival had interrupted, and Bethany went to
sit in a chair near the window. She took off her hat
and laid it in her lap, idly smoothing the plumes
which adorned it, and thinking of what her father
had just said about the Monmouth rebels. All those
she had seen had been simple countrymen like the old
man, Gabriel Penney, whom she had befriended;
beyond all doubt, Jared Vernon did not belong
among them.

Hopson himself brought Vernon from the plantation, hiding certain misgivings beneath a truculent
manner. The summons did not altogether surprise
him, though he had not expected it to come so soon,
and he vented his feelings in the only way he could,
by thrusting the slave before him at pistol-point, and,
when Mr. Court's presence was reached, giving him
so violent a shove forward that he stumbled into the
room and almost measured his length on the floor.

Jared recovered his balance with difficulty and
stood erect, confronting his owner with the arrogant
hostility which had first attracted Bethany's attention. Yet beneath the arrogance, and known only to
himself, seethed a hell of humiliation and futile
anger, for he was acutely conscious of the wretched
appearance he presented, dirty, barefoot and half
naked as he was. Out in the fields, among the other
slaves, he had been able to disregard it, but in this
palatial house; in the presence of the tall, dignified
gentleman in his elegance of silver-laced gray silk
and curled periwig; beneath the compassionate gaze

of the girl whose presence, after one fleeting glance, he did his best to ignore, he tasted a bitterness of mortification such as he had never known. There was a throbbing pain across his shoulders where the overseer's whip had bitten into the flesh, but it was nothing to the agony of spirit he was enduring at that moment.

Mr. Court studied him thoughtfully and then looked at Hopson. "I gave no orders for white servants to be used in the fields," he said sternly, "so why was this man working there?"

"I set the others to work at their own trades, sir, as you bade me," Hopson replied sullenly, "but this fellow has no skill at anything. He could not be left idle."

Mr. Court looked again at Jared. "Is that true?"

"I am a soldier, sir." Jared spoke courteously, but in a voice roughened by an undertone of savage defiance. "I have followed the profession of arms since I was fifteen, and know no other."

"A soldier!" Mr. Court nodded as though this did not surprise him. "Many of our white bond-servants serve in the militia, but a convicted rebel cannot be employed in the defense of the colony. A pity! Our trained soldiers are always too few." Then a sudden thought struck him, and he frowned. "How comes a professional soldier in the rebel army?"

"I am no turncoat, Mr. Court," Jared replied contemptuously. "I left England when I was nineteen, and was for six years in Dutch service, until I left it to follow the Duke of Monmouth."

"You would have done better to stay in Holland," Mr. Court observed dryly. "How came you to Barbados?"

"By the same road, sir, as many of my fellow rebels. I was taken prisoner after our defeat at Sedgemoor, and confined in Ilchester gaol. From there we were marched to Wells for trial, and thence to Weymouth to board the *Happy Return*." Beneath the matted beard, his lips twisted in bitter irony. "Small hope of any return at all for the prisoners *she* bore from England."

Bethany was startled to hear Jared Vernon voice the thought which had entered her own mind as soon as she heard the name of the ship, for the cruel mockery of it seemed to have occurred to no one else. She glanced at her father, but to her surpirse he pursued his inquiries no further. After studying Vernon in silence for a moment or two, he said abruptly to Hopson:

"Set this man to work in the mill. See to it that he is instructed in the processes by which the sugar is refined, and inform me of his progress." To Jared he added, not unkindly: "Since it is impossible for you to practice here the only trade you know, you must of necessity learn another. It will, at least, be better than laboring in the fields."

"My thanks to you, sir," Jared replied, but gratitude was in the words and not the tone. For the first time since entering the room he looked directly at Bethany, and made her a little bow. "To you also, madam."

She inclined her head in response, regarding him with frank sympathy, and felt absurdly disappointed because the gray eyes remained hard and hostile. Yet had she not known all along that one would look in vain for gratitude from this man who seemed to regard the whole world as his enemy?

Hopson was thrusting him once more towards the door when her father spoke again. "A moment! Vernon, your family and friends must be greatly anxious on your behalf. It may be that I can arrange for them to have news of you."

Jared turned again to face him; his voice was courteous but cold. "You are very good, sir, but I have no living kin."

Mr. Court's brows lifted. "No friends, either?"

Again that bitter, mirthless movement of the bearded lips. "Only my companions in misfortune, sir, and they know only too well how I am faring."

There was a pause, then Mr. Court nodded to Hopson to take him away, and as Bethany watched him go she was filled with a compassion so overwhelming that it moved her almost to tears. What was it like, she thought pityingly, to be utterly alone in the world and in such depths of adversity as Jared Vernon now suffered? Surely even the most self-sufficient of men must feel the need of a bond with some other living being; to know that someone cared what became of him?

"He told us very little," she remarked after a pause. "I was surprised, sir, that you did not question him more closely."

"I judged it prudent not to." He saw that she looked puzzled, and went on: "Monmouth's army was composed largely of untrained men. An experienced soldier like Vernon would not have been serving in the ranks, and he has, moreover, the manner of one accustomed to command. I have no doubt he was an officer; if he has been in Dutch service he might even have accompanied Monmouth from Holland. Either fact would be sufficient to hang him. If it were not discovered in England, or if by some oversight he were sent into slavery instead of to the gallows, it were better that I have no knowledge of it."

"I understand," Bethany said slowly. "If you did have such knowledge you could not ignore it, and he might find himself in an even worse plight than at present."

Mr. Court nodded. "Yes, and I have no wish to add to his tribulations. Servitude must be doubly galling to a man of his class, but he is a convicted rebel and the sentence passed upon him has to be carried out. I will do what I can for him, but if ever I saw an intransigent spirit, I see it in that young man."

"Ten years!" Bethany said in a low voice. "Ten years in slavery."

Even spoken aloud it was a length of time almost beyond her power to imagine. It stretched like an eternity, more than half her own life-span, for she was only just seventeen; and if it seemed an eternity to her, free and happy and beloved, what must it seem like to Jared Vernon? Ten years of menial labor; of being penned each night in the stockade, that collection of squalid huts like a village within its high, encircling fence; ten years at the mercy of Will Hopson and his underlings, with the threat of the lash, or worse, as punishment for the smallest defiance. She recalled how he had turned upon Hopson when the overseer struck him, and found herself wondering anxiously how long it would be before he was again provoked beyond endurance.

Her father, watching her, saw the trouble in her face. He got up and came to stand beside her, laying his hand on her shoulder.

"Bethany!" he said quietly. "My dear child, you are allowing these matters to weigh too heavily upon you. Slavery exists. It is upon slave labor that the prosperity of this colony is built, and we cannot do without it. You must learn to accept that."

"I think I do accept it," she said slowly. "I loathe it, and the suffering it causes, but know it is a part of our life here, as much a part as the hurricanes which at times wreak such havoc. I accept it where the Negroes are concerned, and the white men and women who have committed crimes and must be punished, but not for these rebels-convict. Men like old Gabriel Penney, and that poor, frightened boy, and Jared Vernon. Of what are they guilty, save of fighting for what they believe in, of defending the

Protestant faith against Popery? Yet they are sentenced to a term of servitude twice as long as that inflicted upon a thief or a forger. It is the injustice, the inhumanity of it that appalls me."

Just how great that injustice could be she was soon to learn. Her curiosity concerning Jared Vernon was by no means satisfied, so, remembering that she had first seen Gabriel Penney in Jared's company, she decided to question the old man. She had caused him to be given work in the garden, and, finding him there, she greeted him pleasantly, then, having received a respectful reply, said casually:

"What can you tell me, Gabriel, of the man named Jared Vernon?"

He seemed to hesitate, giving her a wary glance, before saying reluctantly: "Little enough, mistress, save that he were shipped here as a slave, same as the rest on us."

"You did not know him, then, before the rebellion?"

"Nay, mistress! The first time I set eyes on Mr. Vernon were in Ilchester gaol. Then we was taken to Wells, and after that they marched us to Weymouth, and a weary way it were. Them too sick to walk was flung into carts, but the rest on us made what shift we could. I'd have died by the roadside but for Mr. Vernon, for I be too old for such marches as that."

"Yet not too old to fight in the rebel army?"

The white head was slowly shaken. "I were never out wi' Monmouth, Miss Bethany. My grandson were, for all I pleaded with him to bide home, wi' harvest-time coming on and all. We was farmers, ye see, Bridgwater way. I swore that if he went he'd not set foot in my house again, but when he did come back, so weary, and wounded, how could I turn him away? Then the King's soldiers come, and carried us both off to gaol."

"But if you had taken no part in the rebellion,"

Bethany said indignantly, "upon what charge did they arrest you?"

"Because I'd given shelter to the lad. 'Knowingly harboring a rebel,' they called it, and said it made me as guilty as him. That be the Law, mistress, seemingly."

"That is monstrous!" Bethany said in a horrified tone. "To treat you as a criminal, simply for caring for your own! How can such a thing be possible in a Christian country?" She looked pityingly at the old man, knowing beyond all doubt that he would never live to see the end of his sentence. "You have been shamefully used, Gabriel, but be sure that *I* shall do all I can to aid you. As for Mr. Vernon, the best counsel you can give him is to curb his temper and his natural resentment, for to give rein to either can only make his situation worse."

She had no means of knowing whether or not Gabriel passed on this excellent advice, and even if he did so, she reflected ruefully, there was probably little hope of it being taken. Jared Vernon did not appear to be the sort of man who would ever pay much heed to advice, or who would obey for long the dictates of caution. Yet if he persisted in his arrogant attitude, he would suffer appallingly. Hopson already resented him, and the head overseer was not a man to let a grudge go unsatisfied.

She found that she could not put the thought of Jared Vernon out of her mind. Her compassion extended to all the slaves, but, just as Jared was different from his fellows, so her concern for him was different also, sharper and more personal than she had ever felt before, and her desire to help him was correspondingly greater.

Two

The date set for Bethany's marriage to Pierce Warren was barely six weeks away. Already Courtlands was growing busy with preparations for the wedding, and through these Bethany herself moved serenely, in no way flustered by her approaching bridal. She had grown up accepting her eventual marriage to Pierce as a natural part of life; something which would happen one day and which provoked in her neither excitement nor dismay. Even now her strongest emotion was concern for her father and sister, for she was mistress of Courtlands and now that she was so soon to leave her home she wondered anxiously how it would fare in Esther's hands. Gentle, self-effacing Esther, who shrank from any responsibility and had never made the slightest attempt to share in her twin's duties.

Bethany was anxious too, about Esther herself. Always reserved to the point of secretiveness, she seemed now to have withdrawn into herself even

more completely. Though they had never been
particularly close, Bethany had always felt protec-
tive, almost maternal, towards her sister, and feared
now that Esther resented the coming marriage when
she herself was not even betrothed. This would not
have mattered had she been a year or two younger,
but since they were twins, it must be galling to her
pride. Several times Bethany tried to bridge the gulf
which seemed to be widening between them, but
every overture was resentfully repulsed and eventually she gave up in despair.

One morning when the two girls sat sewing in a
spacious, handsomely furnished room overlooking
the garden, Pierce arrived, and was shown in by one
of the house-slaves. His visit was unexpected, and
one glance at his haggard face told Bethany that he
brought bad news. She jumped up and went to him
with outstretched hands.

"Pierce, what is it? What has happened?"

"My father!" He took her hands, holding them
tightly with a kind of desperation. "He suffered a
seizure early this morning. Bethany, he is dead!"

"Oh, my dear!" Compassion for his distress, and
the desire to comfort him, transcended even her own
shock. "Come, sit down! Esther, send someone to find
Father."

Esther, who had also risen to stand staring in a
stunned fashion at Pierce, nodded wordlessly and
hurried from the room. Bethany drew Pierce to sit
with her on the day-bed near the window.

"This is a terrible shock," she said in a low voice.
"He seemed so hale and strong!"

He nodded. "I know! I still cannot believe it! Only
yesterday he was speaking of his plans for the
coming year, of clearing more land . . . !" He broke off
abruptly and buried his face in his hands. "Bethany,
what am I to do?"

She put her arm around his hunched shoulders,

holding him close. Her heart ached for his distress, and for the fear and uncertainty those latter words revealed. Pierce was nineteen, but his life hitherto had been singularly carefree, for his father had kept the reins of the estate jealously in his own hands. As the only son, Pierce had been taught all that a plantation owner needed to know, but he had never been given an opportunity to make use of his knowledge or to take any decisions, and now he was appalled by the weight of responsibility thrust so suddenly and dreadfully upon him. To his grief for his father was added increasing panic at the thought of his own new position as head of the family.

"Your poor mother and sisters!" Bethany spoke gently, seeking to turn his thoughts away from himself. "Pierce, you must be strong, for their sake."

He noddedly wretchedly, without looking up. "God knows I want to! I should be with them now, yet I could not bring myself to stay. Despise me for a coward, if you will! I despise myself!"

"Then you must not," she replied softly. "It is the cruel shock of this tragedy which makes you feel like that, but when you have recovered a little from it you will find the strength you need."

He sighed, and groped for her hand to press it to his lips. "With your help I might! Never alone!"

"But you are not alone, Pierce. Or only for a very little while, until we are wed."

"A little while!" He raised his head at last, looking at her with haggard eyes. "Bethany, you have not thought what this means. Our wedding will have to be postponed."

She stared at him in dismay, for this had not occurred to her. Yet she knew it was inevitable. The death of the head of a family meant a long period of deep mourning for his widow and children, during which there could be no thought of such festive occasions as weddings.

"I had forgotten," she said in a low voice. "It will be a year now before our wedding can take place."

Pierce groaned, watching her with hungry eyes. "A year! It will seem like a lifetime! Bethany, my beautiful Bethany, how can I bear to wait so long?"

He caught her in his arms, kissing her more ardently than he had ever done before, for hitherto he had been careful to keep his feelings under rigid control. All his life, in spite of his two years' seniority, he had stood very slightly in awe of Bethany Court, and even after their betrothal had never dared to give rein to the passion she aroused in him. Now, his emotions taut and raw from the shock of his father's death, he was no longer capable of disguising it. He crushed her possessively against him, his lips seeking hers with desperate hunger, and Bethany, after one instant of startled withdrawal, allowed the need to comfort him to overcome her instinctive resistance.

Neither of them was aware that Esther, moving quietly as she always did, had reappeared in the doorway. She halted there, watching them with an expression of distaste and something, too, of bitterness, and then she turned and went away as softly as she had come.

It was not long before heavier footsteps heralded the approach of Matthew Court, and in some confusion Pierce released Bethany and rose hastily to his feet as her father entered the room. Mr. Court came across and gripped him by the hand.

"This is grievous news you bring, Pierce," he said gravely. "It was good of you to spare the time to come yourself."

"I would not send word by a servant, sir," Pierce replied. "Bethany has the right to hear such news from me."

He did not look at her as he spoke, for the half-truth shamed him even as he uttered it, but he could not reveal his doubts and fears to Matthew Court as he had revealed them to her. The elder man nodded.

"Yes, this means that all thought of your wedding must for the present be set aside. It cannot take place while your family is in mourning." He sighed heavily, for he and Mr. Warren had been friends for many years. "This is a sad loss to the whole colony, Pierce, as well as to you and your mother and sisters."

"Father!" Bethany had recovered her composure, and now rose to her feet to stand at Pierce's side. "With your permission, I should like to go with Pierce when he returns home. I may be of some use to Mrs. Warren."

He nodded approvingly. "A good thought, my child. The poor lady will be in need of comforting." He looked at Pierce. "Shall I come also? There will be many sad duties to attend to."

"I would be most grateful, sir." Pierce spoke with frank relief. "I confess that as yet I have scarcely given thought to such matters."

"That is natural enough. Give me a little while to set certain matters here in order, and I will be ready to ride with you."

He went out, and after a minute or two Bethany followed, to make her own preparations. Pierce, left alone, walked across to the window and stood staring unseeingly into the garden, the weight of his loss, forgotten while he held Bethany in his arms, overwhelming him again. The whisper of a footstep on the polished floor failed to rouse him, and he turned with a start as Esther, appearing suddenly at his side, laid a timid hand on his arm.

"I am so sorry, Pierce," she murmured. "So very, very sorry. Bethany sent me away before I could tell you, but I want you to know."

Looking down into the pale face raised so earnestly towards his, he was touched to see that she had been crying. He was fond of Esther in a casual, good-natured way, and occasionally, when something happened to bring the difference between the two sisters forcibly to his attention, pitied her for being so unlike Bethany. He patted her hand in a brotherly fashion.

"I do know, Esther," he said quietly, "and I thank you."

"I wish I could do something to help," she said wistfully, "but that is folly, for Bethany goes with you, does she not? No one ever needs me when she is there."

"Bethany is to be my wife," he reminded her gently.

"Yes! Yes, of course! It is her duty, and her right." Esther's words came even more breathlessly than usual. "I did not mean ...! Besides, she is so capable. She always knows just what should be done. Pierce, you will not tell her what I said?"

"No, of course not. Esther, I sometimes think you are afraid of her."

"Oh, how could I be? I admire her so much, for she is all that I can never hope to be, yet so patient with my own shortcomings. She will be a great comfort to your mother at this sorrowful time, for she will take everything upon her own shoulders. Only think how she has managed this household since our own mother died. She is the most capable person I have ever known."

Bethany stayed at Warrenfield for a week. Esther had been right in supposing that Mrs. Warren would be glad of her presence, for the widow was a gentle, ineffectual woman who had been dependent for every thought and action upon her strong-willed husband, and her sudden bereavement had left her helpless and bewildered. The eldest of her own three daughters was little more than a child, and so she clung the more closely to Bethany during those first lost and sorrowing days of her widowhood. She was reluctant to let the girl go, and when at length Bethany left to return to her own home, begged her to come back soon.

Bethany promised to do so readily enough, eager to do all she could to help and thankful that there was this, at least, she could do for Pierce even though she could not yet become his wife.

During the next few months she paid many lengthy visits to Warrenfield, but though Mrs. Warren came to depend upon her more and more, it sometimes seemed to Bethany that she and Pierce were growing ever farther apart. His new responsibilities weighed heavily upon him, and he tried to disguise his uncertainty with a hectoring manner which grated upon her, and soon lost him the respect of his servants. When Bethany tried to remonstrate with him he grew irritable, and they quarreled frequently. None of their disagreements was particularly serious, but their accumulated effect began to put a strain on the relationship between them, and scandalized Mrs. Warren. She tried not to interfere, but one day, when after a heated exchange Pierce stormed out of the house in a fury, she said tentatively:

"Bethany, my dear, you should not argue so with Pierce. It is not seemly."

"Why not, madam?" Bethany's cheeks were still flushed with temper, and her eyes flashing. "Why not, if I believe him to be in the wrong?"

Mrs. Warren looked more shocked than ever. "It is a man's right to make all decisions, and a woman's duty to abide by them. In more than twenty years of marriage, I never once questioned Mr. Warren's judgment."

Bethany could believe this, and reflected that Pierce was beginning to display the same autocratic ways as his father. "You have a more compliant nature than I, madam," she replied, forcing herself to speak lightly, "but pray do not disturb yourself. Pierce and I understand one another better than you suppose."

Yet even as she spoke, she knew that this was no longer true. She was far less confident of the future than she pretended, and the serene assurance with which she had once contemplated her marriage was troubled now by many doubts. Pierce had changed. If new responsibility worried him, new authority had gone to his head, and the jealous, possessive streak which had always been present in his nature was growing steadily more dominant. It sometimes seemed to Bethany that he treated her as though he owned her, and she resented this the more bitterly because she had for several years enjoyed more freedom than was usually granted to a girl of her age.

She was honest enough, however, to admit to herself that the trouble was not only that Pierce had changed, but that she had not. Her feelings towards him were as they had always been. His desire for her, first betrayed on the day his father died, awoke no response, and his kisses had to be endured rather than enjoyed. She avoided them whenever possible, and thought apprehensively of the coming time when she would no longer have the right to do so. Inevitably, Pierce soon grew impatient of this deliberate elusiveness, and at length, during one of her visits to Warrenfield, challenged her to justify it.

"Bethany, what ails you?" he demanded irritably. "Why do you so persistently avoid being alone with me? And do not prate to me of what is or is not proper! We have spent time enough together in the past."

"When we were young enough for it to be of no consequence. We are not children now."

"No, by God! We are not," he said in a low voice, and pulled her into his arms, covering her face and throat with kisses until with difficulty she thrust him away.

"You ask why I avoid you," she said breathlessly. "Find the answer to that question in your own conduct."

"Devil take it! We are betrothed, and but for the most cursed ill luck would be man and wife."

"Which we cannot be for another six months and more. I think sometimes you forget that."

He thought then that he understood, and was instantly contrite. "Sweetheart, have I frightened you? But you must not be afraid of me, Bethany, for I would never do anything to hurt you. I love you too much." He set his hands on her shoulders, bare above the fashionably low-cut gown, and looked earnestly into her face. "Believe that, and forgive me."

"Of course, Pierce," she replied quietly, but slipped from beneath his caressing touch and moved away. "I think, though, that it might be better if I spent less time at Warrenfield while your family is in mourning."

He scowled, angered by her withdrawal and deliberately misunderstanding her. "To be sure, a house in mourning is a dull place! Not like Courtlands, so near Bridgetown, and with all your father's guests to amuse you. Mr. Court is noted for his hospitality, is he not?"

"Pierce, you know that is not why...!" she was beginning, but he did not stay to hear the rest of her protest. The door slammed behind him, and Bethany sighed. She had tried to bear patiently with his moods, knowing how much she was herself to blame, but she found it impossible to pretend emotions which she did not feel. The fact that she was genuinely fond of Pierce only made the situation worse, for she knew that her attitude hurt him, and hated herself for it.

Nevertheless, that disagreement might have

passed, as their disagreements usually did, but for something which happened the following day. Mr. Warren had purchased several of the rebels-convict, and like Matthew Court, employed them in the more skilled work of the plantation, but one of them, a burly, simple-minded fellow, had proved incapable of anything but the most menial field-labor. So to this he was set, in company with the Negro slaves imported from Africa, and for months had stoically endured the grueling work which lasted from sunrise to sunset, the pitiless heat and the overseer's whip. At last even his dumb endurance broke; he struck down one of his tormentors and fled into the dense forest which fringed the far edges of the cane-fields. Inevitably he was hunted down, and inevitably suffered the merciless flogging which was the usual penalty for attempted escape, yet which, in this instance, did bring escape of a kind, for he died beneath the lash.

Bethany learned of the incident and was unable to restrain her horror and anger. Pierce, trying to defend what had happened, only made matters worse.

"The fellow tried to escape, Bethany, and half killed one of my overseers in doing so. He had to be punished."

"By being beaten to death?"

"His death was not intended, but better that than that he should go unpunished and so risk an uprising. That is a danger never far away."

"Is that any wonder," she retorted bitterly, "when we treat them worse than animals? And the white servants suffer even more than the Negroes, Pierce. You know that!"

He could not deny this. A Negro slave, and his issue, belonged to his master for ever and so was as valuable as any other livestock, but a white servant was bound only for a prescribed number of years.

Pierce could not deny it, but he felt irritably that it was irrelevant to the argument.

"We must have slaves to work the plantations, and while we have slaves we must have strict discipline among them. I have told you before, Bethany, that these are matters in which no woman should meddle, and you had best learn now that you will not be permitted to do so here, no matter what you may have been accustomed to do at Courtlands."

This, as he should have known, was not the tone to take with Bethany Court. Her quick temper flared, and in the ensuing quarrel things were said which were to rankle for a long time. For the sake of appearances and their own dignity they achieved a kind of truce in the end, but that day marked a turning-point in their relationship, which was never to be quite the same again.

Bethany spent a sleepless night, and next morning made an excuse to cut short her visit and return home. Pierce escorted her; they treated each other with studied politeness, but rode for the most part in frigid silence, speaking only when this was unavoidable, and then as briefly as possible.

So they came at length to Courtlands, and as they rode up to the door Esther came out to meet them. She had observed their approach and, being surprised at her sister's unexpected return, came anxiously to discover the reason for it. Pierce dismounted, but before he could help Bethany from the saddle, Gabriel Penney came at a stumbling run through the garden.

"Miss Bethany, praise be you've come back!" he panted as he reached them. "I tried to get word wi' the master, but the blackamoors say he be from home."

Bethany frowned. "What is wrong, Gabriel?"

"It be Mr. Vernon, mistress!" The old man was

gripping her horse's bridle, his breath coming in painful gasps. "That devil Hopson flogged him this morning, and left him bound to the whipping-post, wi' orders that none should free him, or give him food or drink. 'Twill kill him to be left there. In pity's name, Miss Bethany, order him set free!"

She stared at him in horrified dismay. "In God's name, what has he done to merit such punishment?"

Gabriel made a hopeless gesture. "It happened at sunrise, mistress, as they was being marched out to the fields..."

"To the fields?" she interrupted sharply. "My father sent Jared Vernon to work in the mill."

"Aye, mistress, but Mr. Hopson said he were mutinous, and a trouble-maker, and persuaded the master to send him back to field work. That were nigh on two months ago. Always baiting Mr. Vernon, he be, and mocking him afore the rest of us, and today the poor young gentleman couldn't stand it no longer. He knocked Hopson down, and might ha' done more if the other overseers hadn't made him prisoner. That were all the excuse Hopson needed. What he've been hoping for all along."

"I can well believe that," Bethany said bitterly. "Wait here, Gabriel. I shall want to hear more of this presently."

She wheeled her horse about and urged it in the direction of the stockade half a mile away. Pierce called angrily to her to come back, but instead of obeying she spurred her mount to a gallop, conscious of a sense of urgency which would brook no argument.

She thought of the cause of her quarrel with Pierce, and it seemed to her that the same pattern was being hideously repeated; she could only pray that it would not have the same tragic ending. If it did, it would be in some obscure way a defeat; a weapon put into Pierce's hands to prove that her efforts on behalf of the slaves were unavailing, since even on her own father's plantation she was powerless to prevent a man from being beaten to death for a trivial offence.

The gate of the stockade stood open during the day, and Bethany rode straight in, to the consternation of an overseer who was directing two Negroes as they repaired the roof of one of the huts. All three turned to gape at her, but she was scarcely aware of them; she was staring towards the whipping-post which, full in the glare of the sun, stood in the open space in the midst of the stockade. The shock of what she saw there struck her like a blow, so that for a moment she felt physically sick.

The post was a single, sturdy upright of rough-hewn timber with, at its top, a short crossbar to which the hands of the unfortunate slave undergoing punishment could be bound, and in these bonds Jared Vernon now hung, supported only by the ropes about his wrists. On his naked back, from neck to waist, the marks of the lash formed a hideous criss-cross pattern which still bled sluggishly here and there, and upon and around him swarmed tormenting clouds of flies.

Pity and horror helped Bethany to overcome her faintness. She rode forward and leaned across to tug at the ropes, then, finding this useless, turned imperiously to the staring overseer.

"Set this man free!"

He took a couple of paces towards her and then halted in miserable uncertainty. "Miss Court, Mr. Hopson gave orders he is to stay there."

"And I am ordering you to free him! Do the commands of a mere hired servant carry more weight than mine? Free him, I say!"

The anger in her voice, and blazing at him from her blue eyes, convinced the man of the wisdom of obedience. He came forward, drawing out a knife, and Bethany reined back to let him reach the

prisoner. She flung another command to one of the
Negroes.

"Fetch some water! Hasten!"

With unquestioning obedience he loped away, and
Bethany slid from the saddle, beckoning to his fellow
to hold her horse. She was desperately afraid that she
had come too late, for Jared had shown no sign of life,
and when she thought of the hours he must have
stood there under the searing rays of the sun, it
seemed impossible that he could have survived. As
she watched the overseer hacking at the ropes her
anger and compassion were so profound that she
could have wept. It no longer mattered whether or not
she triumphed over Pierce, or vindicated her own
beliefs; her whole concern now was for the man
himself.

The last strand of rope parted; he slumped to his
knees to huddle at the foot of the post, still supported
against it, and the movement jerked a shuddering
groan from his lips. Bethany gave a gasp of relief.

"He is alive!" she exclaimed, and at once became
brisk, turning to the overseer. "Take off your coat and
cover his back with it. That will have to serve until
his hurts can be dressed."

Sullenly he obeyed. Jared uttered a cry of agony as
the garment was laid across his shoulders, and
Bethany flinched in sympathy, but she realized the
urgent need to protect his injuries from the sun and
the flies. His wrists were bleeding, too, where the
ropes had cut into them. As long as his strength
lasted he must have fought like a madman to escape
from those torturing bonds.

The Negro returned with a pannikin of water, and,
taking it from him, she knelt on the dusty ground
beside Jared and held it to his lips. He drank greedily,
and it seemed to revive him, for the gray eyes opened
suddenly and looked straight into hers, so short a
distance away. At first they were blank and dull with

pain, but slowly a kind of astonished recognition dawned in them and his lips moved soundlessly.

"Do not try to speak," she said gently. "You will be cared for now."

Another rider dashed into the stockade. Pierce flung himself from the saddle and strode up to them.

"Bethany, have you run mad? What the devil do you think you are doing?"

She did not even look up at him. With the remaining water she had moistened her costly laced handkerchief and was bathing Jared's face.

"I am doing what I can to relieve the suffering inflicted on this man in my father's name," she said quietly.

"Then it is for your father to deal with if he chooses. I have warned you before of the folly of interfering in the discipline of the stockade."

She did look up at that, a flashing glance of anger and contempt. "Discipline? This is sheer, cold-blooded torture! You may permit such atrocities to be committed on your plantation, Pierce, but my father would never knowingly allow it on his."

Pierce went white with anger. He would have resented such words from her at any time, but now, spoken in front of the overseer and the two staring Negroes, they were intolerable. He caught her by the arm and dragged her roughly to her feet.

"He would not knowingly allow you to demean yourself in this fashion! You have set the rogue free. Let that content you." To the overseer he added: "Have the blacks fling him into his hut."

"So that he may die of fever and neglected wounds?" Bethany struck Pierce's hand aside, but in contrast to the violence of the gesture her voice was dangerously quiet. She turned to the overseer. "You will convey him to the house. I wish to be sure that he is properly cared for."

He looked disbelieving, and glanced at Pierce as

though seeking confirmation of this incredible command. Bethany intercepted the look.

"Mr. Warren is not concerned in this," she said calmly. "I shall tell my father that you acted on my orders, so you have nothing to fear. Pray do as I bid you."

With an apologetic glance at Pierce the man summoned the Negroes and told them to prepare a litter, for it was obvious that Jared was not capable of walking. Pierce looked at Bethany.

"Now I know that you are mad," he said bitterly. "Do you suppose that even your father's indulgence will go to the length of allowing a filthy slave to be sheltered in his house? Do you not realize that you are undermining his authority, and making him ridiculous in the eyes of his servants?"

"There is nothing ridiculous in showing compassion for a fellow being," she replied coldly. "Of course it is for my father to deal with this matter, but until he does, I do not intend to leave Jared Vernon here at the mercy of the man who has already nearly killed him."

"And who will probably find an excuse to do so in truth as soon as the fellow is returned to the stockade," Pierce said dryly. "Do you imagine that in the long run even Vernon himself will have any cause to thank you?"

"It is my hope that after what has happened today, Hopson will be dismissed. It must surely convince my father at last that he is untrustworthy."

He tried to reason with her, but without success. She did not argue, but simply brushed past him and called the overseer to help her mount her horse. Then, without waiting to learn whether or not Pierce would follow, rode quickly back to the house.

Summoning Tabitha and two other female slaves, she set about making preparations to receive the injured man, infecting her helpers with her own sense of urgency to such good effect that by the time Jared was borne into the house, all was in readiness. Bethany watched the Negroes lay him prone on the bed, and then, dismissing them, stood for a moment or two looking down at him, her eyes bright with anger and with pity. Tabitha removed the shielding coat, laying bare again Hopson's hideous handiwork.

"He is to have the best of care, Tabitha," Bethany said at length. "Come to me for anything you need, and if you think his hurts are beyond your skill, tell me, and I will send to Bridgetown for a surgeon. We will do all we can to ease him, but I fear he has much suffering yet to endure."

Pierce had followed Bethany back to the house, but by the time he reached it she had disappeared, and it was left to Esther to see that refreshment was provided for him, and to try to soothe his ill temper. She listened patiently to his complaints against her sister, and when at last he paused, said in her diffident way:

"It is not the least use to criticize Bethany, Pierce, and you should know by now that to do so only makes her the more determined. You will never change her. Perhaps it would be better if you did not try."

"What, when is means that unless I do, I shall never be completely master in my own house? When, every time a slave is chastised, she will want to cosset and pamper him? I can only hope that this latest prank will make your father see the folly of indulging her whims, and that when he comes home he will have that damned rebel flung out of the house."

The hope was not to be realized. By the time Mr. Court returned from Bridgetown, Bethany had gathered a formidable array of facts to lay before him. Most of them she had learned from Gabriel, but

she had also questioned some of the rebels-convict
who worked in the sugar-mill, and from her inquiries
emerged a picture of deliberate and ceaseless persecu-
tion which her father could not ignore.

The key to it lay in the nature of the head overseer.
Will Hopson was a man who hated everyone set by
birth or fortune above him, but circumstances
obliged him to cloak that hatred with servility, and
its only outlet lay in tyrannizing over the wretched
slaves in his charge. He reveled in the terror he
inspired in them. In Jared Vernon he had found a
man who would not be cowed; in whom he recognized
a member of the class he hated, but who, in spite of
that, was completely in his power. From the moment
that fact dawned upon him, Jared was singled out as
a victim. Every menial and degrading task had been
heaped upon him; no opportunity missed of holding
him up to ridicule before his fellow slaves; and when
his temper rose in protest, he was dubbed dangerously mutinous and sent back to the deadly, soul-
destroying labor of the open fields.

"How could you do it, Father?" Bethany demanded fiercely. "How *could* you let Hopson convince you it was necessary, without inquiring further
into the matter? Oh, if only I had known!"

"I kept it from you, child, because I knew it would
distress you. Perhaps I was over-hasty. From what
you tell me it certainly seems that Hopson exceeded
his duty where Vernon is concerned."

"Exceeded his duty?" she repeated bitterly. "Is
that how one describes flogging a man half to death
and then leaving him to the torture of sun and flies?
Hopson is evil, and loves cruelty for its own sake. Sir,
you *must* dismiss him!"

To her dismay, this demand met with a refusal
against which all her arguments were unsuccessful.
Mr. Court would not dismiss Hopson, since free white

servants were hard to come by, though he did agree to remove him from the post of head overseer to a subordinate position, and to bring in a new man to fill the vacant place.

Farther than this Mr. Court refused to go, and Bethany had to accept it, though she was far from content. "That will ease the lot of the slaves in general, and I am glad of it, but what of Jared Vernon, when he recovers? Hopson is not likely to forget he was the cause of his own disfavor."

Her father frowned. "That is true. Confound Vernon! I begin to wish I had never clapped eyes on him, for I am reluctant to send him back to the fields and yet I can think of no other employment for him. He showed little aptitude for work in the mill."

"Did you really expect, sir, that he would?" she said with a sigh. "A gentleman and a soldier?" She was silent for a little while, and then added thoughtfully: "What of the stables? I know he would still be quartered in the stockade, but he would not be working under Hopson, and you have often said that you would be glad to have a white groom, if a suitable man could be found."

"So I have, but whether or not young Vernon would be suitable is another matter. His is not, I fancy, a nature which will take kindly to wearing servant's livery. However, it might serve! We can, at least, try it—if he recovers from his injuries."

Jared did recover, due partly to Bethany's rescue of him from the whipping-post, and the care she provided, and partly to his own hardy constitution. Years of soldiering, and, more recently, the pitiless labor in the cane-fields, had accustomed him to injuries and hardship. Had he been left to rot in the filth and squalor of the stockade nothing could have saved him, but in the cool, clean little room in the plantation house, with old Tabitha to nurse him, he fought victoriously through a long nightmare of pain and fever, in which at first his only ally was the blind, unreasoning instinct to remain alive.

It was a week before he was fully conscious of his surroundings, and another before he was on his feet again, but at last, pale and gaunt and walking stiffly, he was taken, by one of the Negro house-slaves, before Matthew Court.

The elder man, watching him approach, could detect no lessening of arrogance in his bearing, but he realized now that this was a natural assurance, born in him and fostered by the authority of military command. Jared could no more cast it off than he could change the color of his eyes, yet it was but an outward token of a spirit which might break but would never bend. Mr. Court, studying him, wondered dubiously whether the man would ever resign himself to his slavery.

He told him of the new duties awaiting him, and then, because he was sorry for the young man and sincerely wished to help him, went on to add advice which he would not normally have troubled to give.

"I am doing what I can for you, Vernon, though it is little enough. You are a slave with nearly ten years' bondage still before you, and I have no power to alter that, but it is for you to choose how heavily or how lightly the burden of slavery weighs upon you. For the present, you will work as a groom in my stables. Later it may be possible to find more congenial employment for you, though I make no promises. Only remember this! Insubordination of any kind will mean, at the very least, a return to the cane-fields."

Jared thanked him courteously. For the first time in many months he was cleansed and shaven and clad with reasonable decency, and he had sense enough to appreciate the change. In body and in spirit he would bear the scars of the lash for the rest of his life, and though he was resolved, as he had always been, to win somehow to freedom, he had learned that open rebellion was not the way; discretion and patience were far more likely to succeed.

Dismissed by Mr. Court, he was following his fellow slave towards his own quarters again when he came face to face with Bethany, who, not entirely by chance, was passing that way. At once he halted and bowed.

"Madam, is it permitted that I express my gratitude? I am well aware that I owe my life to you."

Bethany had paused also, curiously regarding him, for this was the first time she had seen him without the disfiguring beard. The features now revealed were of a somewhat haughty cast. High cheekbones; thin, high-bridged nose; the lips thin, too, though well-shaped. A keen, intrepid face, the face of an adventurer and a gambler. Not the face or, for that matter, the manner of a slave.

"It is Gabriel Penney to whom your thanks are due," she replied, "for it was he who told me of your plight."

"But you, Miss Court, who freed me from it and saw that I was cared for. It will be my hope and my endeavor to repay that debt some day."

She looked gravely up at him. "I know of no debt," she said quietly, "but if *you* feel that one exists, seek to repay it by ensuring that what I did was not in vain. I want to help you, but I cannot do it in spite of you."

He studied her without speaking, his eyes faintly perplexed but, at last, no longer hostile, and for a few seconds she steadfastly returned that keen regard. Then, before he could find anything to say, she went on her way, quietly self-possessed, yet very much aware that he still stood there, staring after her.

Three

"Esther, are you still determined not to come with me to visit Great-Aunt Elizabeth?" Bethany asked with a hint of reproach. "It is bound to displease her."

"Oh, Bethany, I would much prefer not to! You know I dislike it, and I did come with you last week, and the week before that. Can you not tell her that I am indisposed?"

Bethany looked at her with amused exasperation. "Very well, but it is no wonder she considers you a sickly creature, when you so often invent an indisposition in order to avoid visiting her."

Elizabeth Milford was their only female relative in Barbados. The elderly and autocratic widow of a wealthy shipowner, she lived alone in her fine house on the other side of Bridgetown, where she terrorized her household with her sharp tongue. She hardly ever went out, for she was enormously fat and found the effort of moving around in the tropic heat too great to be borne, and she had alienated all her acquain-

tances with her short temper and barbed remarks.
Bethany visited her dutifully every week, but Esther,
who was terrified of the old lady, avoided going with
her whenever she could.

"I will make your excuses this time," Bethany said
now, "but you do realize, do you not, that when I am
married, you will *have* to visit her every week?"

"I will do my duty when I have to—that is, if
Great-Aunt wishes to see me," Esther assured her.
She hesitated, and then added with even more than
her customary diffidence: "Bethany, you are not still
at odds with Pierce, are you? He was so angry with
you that day you went to the stockade."

"No angrier than I was with him," Bethany
replied lightly, "but we made our peace the next time
we met. Now all is well—until we quarrel again." She
made a little grimace at Esther's look of shocked
reproof. "We *shall* quarrel, so there is no point in
pretending otherwise. I told Pierce once that if he
wanted a docile wife he should be marrying you
instead of me."

She was turning to the door as she spoke, and did
not see the sudden flush which swept across Esther's
face, or the pallor which succeeded it. She went
quickly from the room, for she had no wish to discuss
with Esther the problem of her relationship with
Pierce. She could see no solution to it, and preferred to
put it out of her mind whenever possible.

She did so on this occasion with less difficulty than
usual, for already her thoughts were occupied
elsewhere. Esther's refusal to accompany her provided at last an opportunity she had been seeking for
several weeks, and when she ordered her horse to be
brought round, she added casually that she would
have the English groom, Vernon, to attend her.

Bethany wanted to know more about Jared
Vernon, and thought that she might be able to
persuade him to talk more freely to her than he had

done to her father. There was so much about him which intrigued her, and she was too inexperienced to probe the reason for her curiosity, or to question the wisdom of indulging it.

When she emerged from the house, he was standing with the horses in the shade of a wide-spreading tree near the door. Not even servant's livery could make him look like a servant, and though when he had replied courteously to her greeting, he stooped and linked his hands so that she might place her foot in them and be lifted into the saddle, there was nothing servile in the action. Thus might any gentleman perform the small service for a lady of his acquaintance. Only when he mounted his own horse, and reined back to follow her at a respectful distance towards the road, was the illusion dispelled.

When they had left the plantation behind them she glanced round and beckoned to him. He spurred forward and looked at her in deferential inquiry, with only the faintest glimmer of mockery deep down in his eyes.

"Madam?"

Having summoned him, she could not immediately think of anything to say, and, after an awkward pause, asked lamely: "Have you fully recovered from your injuries?"

"Completely, madam, thank you. That, like so much else, I owe to you. Even the fact that life is no longer entirely a hell upon earth."

She looked searchingly at him. "And you have not fallen foul of Hopson again since your return to the stockade?"

He shook his head. "He pays no heed to me, and the new head overseer, Becket, sees to it that he has little opportunity to work mischief of any kind."

He did not feel it necessary to speak of the brooding hatred he read in Hopson's eyes whenever their paths chanced to cross, or of his own conviction that that

hatred would be loosed again if it could be done
without any unpleasant consequences to Hopson
himself. The man's position now was intolerable. As
head overseer he had played the tyrant with his
subordinates as well as with the slaves, and they
were not slow to take their revenge now that he was
no longer in authority over them. He was free to leave
Matthew Court's service, and that he did not seemed
to Jared a clear indication that he sought to avenge
himself upon the authors of his downfall.

"I gave orders," Bethany said after a moment,
"that you were to have a hut to yourself, but Gabriel
tells me that he shares it with you."

"I sought leave for him to do so. Do not think me
ungrateful, Miss Court, but I owe *him* something
also, and he has not long to live." He saw the shocked
dismay in her face, and added harshly: "Death is the
only release he can hope for. Do not let sentiment
blind you to that."

It occurred to neither of them that this was
scarcely a proper way for a slave to address the
daughter of his master. Bethany said in a low voice:

"That poor old man! Is it indeed true that he was
convicted simply because he sheltered his grandson?
It seems scarcely believable."

"It is true!" Jared's tone was grim. "Knowingly to
aid and comfort a rebel is to be guilty of rebellion.
That, madam, is how justice is dispensed by the
bloody-minded tyrant, James, and his Lord Chief
butcher, Jeffreys."

Bethany gasped. "That is treason!"

"Of course!" A sardonic note crept into Jared's
voice. "Am I not already a convicted rebel? Why
should I fear to speak the truth?"

She thought it better not to pursue this. "We have
often wondered," she said diffidently, "how you came
to be transported at all. We were told that only the
rank and file of the rebel army were sent to the

plantations, and all your companions, in fact, are men of the humbler sort."

There was silence for a moment; then he shrugged. "You, at least, have a right to know the truth. I crossed with Monmouth from Holland, and held the rank of Lieutenant-Colonel in his army. Both these facts were made known at my trial and I was condemned to death. But there were many other rebels, such as old Gabriel, whose sentence was ten years' slavery, and all of us were herded together in such conditions that men were dying every day. When it was time for those bound for the plantations to be marched away, an officer came with a list of names which he called one by one, the men so summoned being commanded to stand forth. One of the names was that of a poor fellow whom I knew was at that very moment breathing his last." He paused, and Bethany saw a look of self-mockery come into his face. "When one is under sentence of death, the chance of life, even life in slavery, is all that one desires. I stood forth in his stead."

"And the deception was never discovered?"

"Not to my knowledge. The captain of the *Happy Return* had been ordered to take aboard a certain number of rebels-convict, and when the right number reached him, he inquired no further. Only Gabriel knew the truth, and once we were at sea I could congratulate myself on having cheated the gallows." He laughed shortly, without amusement. "I had little conception then of what slavery would mean."

"You have suffered bitterly," Bethany agreed, "but my father is neither cruel nor unjust, and now that his eyes have been opened to Hopson's villainy, conditions will be better for all the slaves. Even a bond-servant can occupy a position of trust, and you are young and strong. You can have hope, where Gabriel has none."

Watching him, she saw a strange look come into

his face, almost as though a mask had descended
upon it, and she thought with sudden, absolute
certainty, "he will try to escape." The thought
stabbed her with sharp dismay, for any such attempt
was almost certainly foredoomed to failure, and then
no one would have the power to save him. She wanted
to warn him, to urge him to put all thought of escape
from his mind, but even though she was the mistress
and he the slave, she felt that to utter such a warning
would be an impertinence.

"I will do all I can for Gabriel," she said at length,
"but you are right. He fails more rapidly day by day."
She thought of the old man as she had seen him that
morning, moving wearily among the flamboyant
blossoms in her garden, and all her helpless anger,
her loathing of the cruelty and injustice which most
of those around her accepted as normal, welled up
again. "Oh, it is infamous! He did not even support
your rebel Duke. He did no harm to anyone, yet he is
condemned to slavery and sent to die in a strange
land. And that is justice!"

"No," Jared said in a hard voice, "is it the Law,
which is not at all the same thing." He regarded her
for a moment, and then added abruptly: "Miss Court,
I would like to ask your pardon."

"My pardon?" Bethany was startled. "For what?"

"For the harsh thoughts I harbored the first time I
saw you. You will not recall it, but it was on the
waterfront, the day we were brought ashore. You
were mounted on the same black mare you ride today,
and you sat in the shade and watched us, and talked
with the captain of Militia, and then with another
young man. 'An idle fine lady,' I thought, 'beguiling a
tedious hour by staring at a crowd of slaves while she
flirts with her gallants.'" Bethany gasped, turning
an indignant look upon him, and he added apologetically: "What else was I to think? There seemed no
likelihood that anyone on this pestilent island would

spare us even one kindly thought. I have learned since how much I wronged you. That is why I ask you to pardon me."

"Since you admit your error, I will do so," she said with a smile. "So that is why you looked at me with such contempt that day! I confess it puzzled me." She colored faintly, and went on in a slightly defensive tone: "That is what made me notice you. That, and the fact that, alone of all your fellows, you seemed defiant still. Defiant and angry, hating us all."

"When one is being bought and sold like an animal," he said grimly, "hatred is the only thing which keeps at bay the humiliation and the despair. Seeing you reminded me of all that life could never be again, and at that moment, Miss Court, I hated you more than any living being." Then his expression relaxed a little, and a faint smile touched his lips. "Even though you were the fairest sight I had seen for many weary months."

The color in her cheeks deepened to scarlet; she said angrily: "That is enough! You forget yourself!"

"Yes!" Jared's face was suddenly white, his voice bitter. "For a moment I did forget. My apologies, Miss Court."

He dragged his horse violently to a halt and waited until Bethany was again a little distance ahead. For the rest of the way to her great-aunt's house, and later, during the return journey, his manner was rigidly correct. He betrayed no emotion of any kind, and Bethany could only hope that her own bearing was equally impassive. She was angry and distressed, and in some curious way felt that it was she who was in the wrong.

Her conversation with Jared, far from satisfying Bethany's curiosity, merely increased it. Going over it in her mind, she regretted the sharp rebuke which had brought it to an end. He had been impertinent, but it was an impertinence which arose from their respective positions, and not from any impropriety in what he had said; and had she not invited it by her own manner? Her indignation had been out of all proportion to the offense, and might well have driven him again into the bitter hostility which, combined with his reckless temper, had already cost him so dear.

Had she but known it, there was little danger of this. Jared was reckless, but he was not a fool, and he returned to his work in the stables in a thoughtful frame of mind. Bethany had judged correctly his fierce determination to escape, but he had already learned that an escape would need to be carefully planned. To embark on mere headlong flight at the first opportunity was to invite disaster.

Yet to make plans, knowledge was essential, and of the New World he knew nothing at all, nor was there, even in his present improved circumstances, much opportunity to learn. But Bethany Court, who had been born and bred in the Indies, was clearly disposed to be friendly. If he were given another opportunity, if he had not altogether ruined his chances with that spontaneous but ill-judged piece of gallantry, he would be more circumspect in future, and Bethany, in all innocence, would tell him what he needed to know.

When he was next summoned to attend her, her sister rode with them and there was no opportunity for him to offer any apology, but at last, a week or so later, he was again ordered to attend Miss Court when she rode abroad. He waited until they were out of sight of the house, and then, bringing his horse alongside hers, respectfully sought leave to speak. Bethany, who had been trying in vain to think of a way to make amends without too much loss of dignity, gave it readily.

"I wish to offer my apologies, Miss Court, for what I said to you the first time I attended upon you. I spoke in all sincerity and meant no offense, but I am aware that I had no right to speak at all. My only excuse is that the kindness you showed me that day made it all too easy to forget that I am no longer a free man."

She studied him for a moment or two before making any reply. There was a diffidence in his manner, and a hint of entreaty in the gray eyes, which touched her strangely. "I accept your apology," she said quietly at length. "Tell me, does such forgetfulness ease the burden of bondage, or make it heavier to bear when remembrance returns?"

"The relief of torment, madam, is always to be welcomed," he replied wryly, "since it gives renewed strength to endure again."

She nodded slowly, her gaze still searching his face. "Yes, that I can understand. Ride here beside me, then, and we will talk." She paused, and then added with a smile: "But not, if you please, of treasonable matters, for that can profit neither of us."

"I have learned, madam, that treason, unless it be successful, can profit no one. I fear, though, that if we are to talk of England, anything I may say is likely to be treasonable."

"Of what, then?"

He shrugged, concealing the elation he felt. "Of the Indies, if it please you. I know nothing of the New World, but if I am to be bond here for ten years, it were as well to learn."

She found nothing suspicious in the request. Naturally it would be painful to him to speak of his former life, when he had been a free man with hopes and ambitions which might one day be realized but which now had vanished like a pricked bubble. So, though she would have liked to learn more about her mother's native land, she began to talk instead of Barbados, and how the Court family had come to settle there.

"My great-grandfather came to the colony in his youth," she explained. "He was a younger son, and used his modest inheritance to establish a small tobacco plantation. When the cultivation of sugar was introduced he was among the first to adopt the new crop. He prospered, as so many did. Now Courtlands is one of the largest plantations on the island."

Jared nodded. "Even in Europe I heard of the great fortunes which have been made from the cultivation of sugar—though, by my faith, I never thought then to become so intimately and painfully acquainted with that process."

She sighed. "I marvel that you can speak of it so lightly. Great wealth has been amassed, it is true, but at a terrible price in human suffering. In the early days of the colony each settler cultivated his own small piece of land, but when sugar-cane was introduced as a crop, this was no longer practicable. The poorer settlers sold their land to the more prosperous and became mere hired laborers. As the cane-fields grew in size and number, slaves in ever-increasing numbers were brought in to tend them, until today the number of blacks on the island outnumber the whites by many thousand. Yet the death-toll has been enormous." She made a sudden, impatient movement, and her horse, startled, flung up its head. "I am for ever holding forth against the suffering of the slaves, yet all the while I lie soft and wear silk and fine linen because of the wealth purchased with their blood and tears. There are times when I despise myself!"

She spoke with such vehemence that Jared cast her a startled, suspicious glance, but he saw at once that this was no pose, no easy, sentimental sympathy. At a time and in a place where slavery was an accepted fact of life, this young girl, who might have been expected to concern herself only with finery and admirers, cared deeply and passionately for the miseries of her enslaved fellow beings. Jared was already grateful to Bethany Court; in that moment of revelation he began to respect her.

"Yet who would benefit," he said quietly, "if you were to deny yourself these things? Would it do anything to relieve the suffering you loathe so deeply, or give freedom to even one of your father's slaves?"

"It would not, of course," she admitted ruefully. "All it would achieve is the selfish easing of my own tender conscience, and would in itself be a luxury. I fear you are a cynic, Jared Vernon!"

He shook his head. "Not a cynic, madam. A realist. I have never been able to appreciate grand, heroic gestures which benefit no one."

"That is difficult to believe," she replied dryly, "coming from one who risked his life for faith in a rebel cause. From all that I have heard, Monmouth's uprising was just such a gesture as you affect to despise."

"Not to me, Miss Court. I saw it as a gamble wherein, though the stakes were high, the prize made the game worthwhile. Monmouth *might* have triumphed. If he had, the gains of those who had helped him to his throne would have been enormous." He observed her faint frown of disapproval, and a sardonic smile touched his lips. "I am no idealist, madam. I did not offer my sword to Monmouth out of a burning desire to cleanse England of Popery and re-establish the Anglican faith."

"Then why?" she asked reproachfully. "Not, surely, for personal gain alone?"

"For personal gain!" Jared's voice was suddenly hard, and there was a look in his face which made him appear older than his five-and-twenty years.

"Though not, I imagine, gain of the kind you suppose. Let us say that I saw in it a chance to achieve a purpose otherwise impossible to fulfill." He laughed shortly, mocking his own vanished hopes. "A purpose now never likely to be achieved at all."

Bethany would have liked to know more, but some instinct warned her to probe no further. This was a man of unpredictable moods, and she would need to tread warily if she were ever to win his confidence. After a little, she began to talk again about the island and its history, as though no more personal note had ever intruded into the conversation.

They had many such conversations in the weeks which followed, and a curious kind of friendship grew up between them. Soon it was taken for granted in the Courtlands' stable that when Miss Bethany sent for her horse, the English groom would answer the summons. Sometimes Esther rode with them, but on those occasions, and always when they were where others might observe them, he was no more than attentive, unobtrusive servant. When they were alone, however, Bethany would beckon him beside her and they would talk, the horses pacing slowly, the riders utterly absorbed.

They talked of many things, and even argued briskly about some of them, Jared alternately amused and intrigued by his companion's forthright speech and independence of thought. He had never before given much consideration to a woman's mind. Women were to be courted, complimented, made love to and then parted from as lightly as possible, mere delectable incidents in a soldier's adventurous career. His friendship with Bethany was something entirely novel in his experience; deliberately he had set himself to turn her sympathy and liking to his own advantage, and had benefited in a way he had never envisaged. He was beginning to acquire the knowledge he needed, but her companionship had come to mean much more to him than that. It was the one thing which enabled him to endure the endless humiliation and harsh treatment which were the lot of any slave, no matter how favored; the one thing, he felt sometimes, which kept him sane.

Bethany herself found increasing pleasure in their friendship, and if she was at pains to keep it secret, this was for his sake rather than her own. Already he was looked upon with a certain amount of resentment by those rebels-convict who had been purchased with him, and she had no wish to give them added cause for ill feeling towards him. Then, too, she guessed that her father would not approve if he discovered the degree of intimacy which existed between them. He felt sympathy for Jared, but it would not extend to condoning a friendship between his daughter and the English slave. She did not like deceiving him, but somehow it seemed even more important to give Jared all the help and comfort she could.

As yet Mr. Court had no suspicions. He asked her one day if Vernon performed his duties adequately, and whether, in her opinion, he was now resigned to bondage.

Bethany sighed. "I doubt he will ever be that, sir. As to his duties, I have not the smallest complaint to make, and I think he is as content now as he will ever be."

"He is certainly an exceptional horseman," Mr. Court remarked. "I had despaired of ever completely breaking in that bay stallion we bred, but Vernon has gentled him. It was a happy thought, child, to send him to work in the stables."

Pierce regarded the new groom with less favor. He arrived unexpectedly at Courtlands one day, having transacted some business in Bridgetown, to find that Bethany was out riding. Esther, who told him this, did her best to entertain him, but he was inattentive, and the sound of approaching horses took him immediately to the door of the house.

He reached it in time to see Bethany dismount. She kicked her foot free of the stirrup and allowed the tall groom in the Court livery to lift her down. For a moment his hands were about her slender waist, and her own rested lightly on his shoulders as he swung her easily to the ground. Pierce had seen servants perform a similar service for her scores of times and thought nothing of it, but on this occasion it roused in him an illogical anger. He spoke her name, more peremptorily than he had intended, and went quickly towards her.

She swung round at the sound of his voice, smiling and putting out her hand. He took it, and, prompted by an impulse he scarcely understood, pulled her to him and kissed her on the lips.

Bethany was startled and a little displeased. The greeting-kiss was accepted custom even among mere friends, and Pierce had every right to kiss her if he chose, but he was well aware that she had no liking for such casual caresses. She was acutely aware of Jared standing beside them, and was about to bid him lead the horses away when Pierce forestalled her.

"Why the devil are you loitering here?" His voice held the bullying tone she so much disliked. "Get back to the stables, where you belong."

Anger flamed into Jared's eyes, and for one dismayed instant Bethany feared that he would give way to it, but then he bowed to her and, ignoring her companion, led the horses away. Bethany jerked her hand from Pierce's and said in a low, angry voice:

"How dare you? Understand this, Pierce! I will not have my servants spoken to in that way."

He scowled at her, aware that he was in the wrong but made obstinate by that unreasoning anger. He

was not sure what had prompted it. Perhaps it was
Vernon's bearing, which made it so difficult to think
of him as a servant; perhaps the little smile of thanks
Bethany had bestowed on him as he set her down;
perhaps simply the knowledge that, though circumstances had made Jared Vernon a slave, he was a
man older and more experienced and more assured
than Pierce himself.

"Must we now consider our slaves' feelings as well
as pamper their bodies?" he asked with heavy
sarcasm.

Bethany looked at him with scornful reproach.
"Do you think they have none?" she countered
quietly. "That physical suffering is all a man in
Vernon's situation has to endure? It is easy to mock
adversity, Pierce, when one is not obliged to endure
it."

He had the grace to look a little ashamed.
"Perhaps you are right—though in Vernon's case he
suffers adversity through his own fault. But we will
not quarrel over it." He took her hand again, looking
pleadingly at her. "Will you forgive my ill-humor,
Bethany?"

She assented, mainly because it occurred to her
that if Pierce were allowed to cherish animosity
towards Jared, he might find a way to turn her father
against him, and that, for Jared's sake, must at all
costs be avoided.

Jared himself, returning to the stables and
learning from old Joshua, the coachman, who the
bad-tempered visitor was, set about the task of
unsaddling and grooming the horses in a thoughtful frame of mind. The information that Miss
Bethany was betrothed and would, in a few months'
time, be married, made him realize that his own bid
for freedom must be made before her wedding took
place. With Bethany gone from Courtlands, his
liberty was bound to be curtailed, and an opportunity

to escape correspondingly harder to find. It would be
risky enough in any event, a life-and-death gamble
with the odds heavily against him, but it was a risk
he was unshakably determined to take.

As the weeks dragged into months, escape remained his sole ambition, the goal of which nothing
could cause him to lose sight. He listened and
questioned, storing up every particle of information
Bethany let fall, or which he could learn for himself
in the course of his duties, preparing himself
constantly for the attempt which must not fail.
Deliberately he was using her to further his own
ends, and sometimes, in the face of the friendship she
so generously and unhesitatingly offered, he was
troubled by pangs of conscience, but stifled them
with the thought that it were better she should know
nothing of what he was planning to do.

These were not the only feelings which troubled
him where Bethany was concerned. He was too much
aware of her beauty, and there were times when his
longing for her reached an almost unbearable
intensity, but he mastered it with that ruthlessness
which was an essential part of his nature. Her image
might torment him constantly, and those fleeting
contacts when he lifted her from her horse cause his
blood to quicken, but he was resolved that never by
word or look would he betray it. To let her know the
truth; even, perhaps, to rouse in her a like awareness,
would be an act of treachery too vile to contemplate.
To Jared, Bethany was sacrosanct. She would
always hold a unique place in his heart and his
memory, yet when the time came he would leave her;
with regret, certainly, but without hesitation.

Bethany herself was as yet troubled by no
self-questioning. If her happiest hours were those
spent in Jared's company; if he was never, at any

time, far from her thoughts, it did not occur to her to wonder why it should be so. Although by this time she knew him well, he was still, in some ways, as much a mystery as he had been at the outset, for he never spoke of his own personal history. She did not even know from which part of England he came, or whether he had spoken the truth when he told her father that he had no living kin. Nor had he ever referred again to the purpose which had led him to espouse the cause of the Duke of Monmouth. His very reticence whetted her desire to know more, but she could not bring herself to question him. The confidence, if it ever came, must come unsought.

Once he did seem to be on the point of telling her. They were riding back to Courtlands from Government House, whither Bethany had gone to visit the Governor's lady, and Jared was telling her of a certain adventure which had befallen him in Holland. When he came to the end of the story, Bethany said idly:

"Why did you choose to fight for Holland? Would there not have been greater opportunities for advancement in the service of a powerful nation like France?"

There was a long pause, so long that she looked at him in surprise, thinking that he was not going to reply. He was staring straight ahead beneath frowning brows, his expression withdrawn and a trifle forbidding. Then, as though aware of her glance, he said abruptly:

"My mother was Dutch."

Bethany's lips parted in astonishment, but she could think of nothing to say. This might be the beginning of a deeper knowledge and a deeper understanding of him, and she was desperately afraid of doing anything which might prevent it. She wanted such understanding more than she had realized until that moment.

"I did not realize," she ventured at length, when he did not speak again. "I thought you were an Englishman."

"My father was." Jared spoke curtly, almost reluctantly. "He lived in Holland during the years of Cromwell's rule."

He broke off abruptly. They had been so engrossed in talk that they had not heard the sound of approaching hoofbeats, but now they rounded a bend to see another rider coming towards them. Jared swore softly, and Bethany drew rein in involuntary dismay, for after an instant of astonished recognition the newcomer spurred his horse to a gallop and bore down upon them. It was Pierce Warren.

He reined in before them in a cloud of dust, barring the narrow road and looking from one to the other with angry suspicion, his face white with anger. Bethany, as little pleased by the encounter as he was, but disguising the fact more successfully, said with tolerable composure:

"Why, Pierce, what do you here? I did not expect you today."

"I'll wager you did not," he replied unpleasantly. "I went to Courtlands and Esther told me whither you had gone, so I came to meet you. I thought we could ride back together."

"Then let us do so," she replied, and signed to Jared to draw back, but Pierce abruptly intervened.

"Ride on before us," he said curtly to the other man. "Miss Court has no further need of you."

Jared regarded him steadily for a moment and then looked inquiringly at Bethany. She nodded in confirmation of the orders, but softened the dismissal with a smile, and so with a little bow to her he rode off in the direction of the plantation. Pierce watched him go, his expression still dark with anger.

"That fellow would be the better for another

flogging," he said viciously. "He is too damnably insolent."

"I saw no insolence." Bethany still spoke calmly, trying to subdue her annoyance and disappointment that Pierce should have appeared at that particular moment. "He is my father's servant. He expects to take his orders from me."

"Do you always treat your father's servants with such familiarity? Ride with your groom in such close and friendly fashion as you were doing when I surprised you?"

Not trusting herself to reply, she flashed him a glance of contempt and urged her horse forward, but Pierce wheeled his mount and leaned forward to grasp hers by the bridle, bringing it to a halt again.

"Answer me when I question you! Have you no pride, that you condescend so far to an upstart slave?"

"When the 'upstart slave,' as you call him, is an unfortunate gentleman who bears adversity with courage, I see no need for pride *or* condescension."

They glared at each other, both furious now and not attempting to dissemble it. Pierce, who by his very nature suffered torments of jealous doubt where Bethany was concerned, could not bear to see her show even the most commonplace interest in any other man. On this occasion he had not, in the first instant of their encounter, recognized her companion, seeing only a tall man who sat his horse well, and about whom there clung an indefinable air of authority, but that had been enough to bring suspicion leaping into life. A moment later the Court livery had informed him that this was the English slave, Jared Vernon, for whom she had already shown such uncommon concern.

Now it appeared that she did not regard the man in the light of a servant, nor—which was worse—did

Vernon so regard himself, at least where Bethany was concerned. Pierce, recalling the level gaze of those cool gray eyes, fancied that he could also recall mockery in them, and the thought fanned his anger to white heat.

"Unfortunate gentleman!" he repeated jeeringly. "Do you not know that only those rebels of no account were transported? Vernon is no more than an adventurer aping the manners of his betters, and only a foolish girl would be deceived by him."

Bethany, recollecting in time the ruse by which Jared had evaded execution, bit back the angry reply which had risen to her lips. "Oh, Pierce, what ails you? Why do you always try to pick a quarrel with me?"

"Why do you always give me cause?" he retorted. "Last time I came to visit you I found Maynard dallying after you, and now...!"

"You are utterly unreasonable!" she broke in, her temper flaring up again. "Captain Maynard was waiting to see Father. You know that!"

"I know that I found you alone with him!"

She gave a sigh of exasperation. "Esther had been with us until a few moments before you arrived."

"And who was there to chaperon you today 'until a few moments before' I arrived?" he said with a sneer. "You are adept, are you not, at ridding yourself of your sister's tiresome presence?"

"Now you are insulting me!" she said furiously. "I tell you, Pierce, I am weary to death of your jealousy and suspicion. I will not endure it!"

She jerked the bridle from his grasp and flicked her mount with the whip, sending the animal bounding forward. Pierce called angrily to her to wait, but she paid no heed and, although she could hear his horse pounding after her, did not slacken speed until Courtlands was reached. He caught up with her as she was entering the house, and gripped her by the hand.

"Bethany!" His tone was pleading now, but he spoke softly, mindful of the groom—not Jared—who was leading away their horses. "Forgive me! I should not have berated you as I did. It is this damnable waiting which frays my temper! You do not know how I suffer, but everything will be different once we are married. I swear it!"

"Will it?" she asked wearily. "You cannot keep me a prisoner in your house, you know, forbidding any other man to come near me."

"You have every right to rebuke me," he admitted ruefully, "but I love you so much, Bethany! That is why I cannot bear you to look with kindness at another man, even a poor devil of a slave. At least believe that!"

"I do believe it, Pierce," she said with a sigh. "I think you do love me, in your own way."

Yet could there be love without trust, she wondered, and would marriage work the miracle he so confidently predicted? She hoped desperately that he was right, but could not rid herself of doubt; and if the miracle did not happen, how could she endure a lifetime clouded by jealously and groundless suspicion? For the first time in her life, Bethany found herself contemplating the future with a sinking heart.

Four

Bethany, seated on the ground with her back against
the trunk of a tall cabbage-palm, drew patterns in the
sand with her riding-whip, and from time to time
glanced anxiously at Jared, standing beside their
tethered horses a short distance away. He seemed
unusually preoccupied, and all her efforts at conversation during their ride had met with no success. It
was as though he had suddenly withdrawn again
into that forbidding reserve which had marked the
early days of their acquaintance.

She felt curiously rebuffed. They had ridden by one
of her favorite ways, a narrow track through the
fringes of the forest which led at length to this spot by
the shore, where below the green wall of trees and
undergrowth the dazzling white coral sand stretched
in an empty crescent lapped by the sea. They were
alone, secure from curious or condemning eyes, yet he
had uttered scarcely half a dozen words since they

dismounted, but just stood staring out across the sea, one hand idly stroking the black mare's glossy neck.

"Jared!" she said sharply, and because of her hurt and exasperation, her voice held an imperiousness she did not intend. "What ails you today? Is it anything to do with Will Hopson?"

They had encountered the overseer as they skirted the edge of the plantation, and though he had uncovered and bowed with his usual servility, it had seemed to Bethany that he looked at Jared with sly satisfaction, almost with triumph. All her old distrust of the man had been revived by that look.

"No, madam, nothing," Jared replied briefly. He did not want to discuss Hopson with her, for though the man had never dared to make any overt move against him, he had still found a way of taking his revenge upon them both.

For months now there had been lewd rumors afoot among overseers and convicts alike concerning Jared's relationship with Bethany, so that muttered ribaldries and knowing looks followed them whenever they chanced to ride through the plantation. Jared had no doubt that Hopson had started the gossip. He would not be rash enough to slander Bethany directly to her father, but there was every chance that a carefully nourished scandal might in time reach Matthew Court's ears, and then Heaven help the slave with whom her name had been coupled. For Bethany's sake, Jared hoped devoutly that she would never become aware of those insulting rumors; for his own sake he hoped that her father would not.

"What is it, then?" she was insisting now. "You cannot deny that something is troubling you."

"No, I cannot deny it." He walked across and stood looking down at her, his face somber. "Old Gabriel died last night."

She caught her breath in dismay, for though the news had been long expected, it was still a shock. "You were with him?"

"Yes, but he did not know me. At the last he thought I was his grandson, the lad who died of gaol fever at Ilchester before ever we were brought to trial. He had forgotten that, forgotten where he was and all that had befallen him. He thought he was at home in Somerset. I let him believe it. It was kinder so."

Bethany's eyes filled with tears. There was something unbearably poignant in the thought of the old man, dragged from his peaceful farm to the hell of the slave stockade, remembering at the last nothing of the cruelty and injustice inflicted upon him. She bowed her head, whispering a prayer for him, and the tears splashed down on to her clasped hands.

"Do not weep for him!" Jared's voice was harsh, rough with anger and bitterness. "His servitude is over. He is to be envied, not pitied!"

Bethany pressed her fingertips against her closed eyes, forcing herself to remember that Gabriel had been Jared's friend. His only friend among the rebels convict, for the others regarded him with hostility, resentful of his privileged position, his refusal to be cowed by his present circumstances. Now Gabriel was dead, and Jared solitary indeed.

She choked back her tears, taking deep, slow breaths until she was in command of herself again, and then lifted her head to look up at him. He had turned away and was staring out across the sea, his expression a curious blend of bitterness and desperation. Pity stabbed painfully through her; pity, and some other emotion which for a second or two she could not define. Then realization came and she sat very still, seeing, with sudden, blinding self-knowledge, whither the past months had been leading her. Looking at Jared, and thinking, with utter simplicity and utter conviction, "this is my love."

"Not yet one year!" The sound of his voice made her start, but he was still looking seaward and seemed unaware that he had spoken aloud. "One year out of ten!"

She did not need to be told what he was thinking. It had been in his mind all along, and now Gabriel's death had acted as a spur to the desperate resolve. He would attempt escape and, like those who had attempted it before him, achieve only his own destruction. Escape and recapture! An appallingly vivid picture of what that would mean flashed, unsought and horrifying, into her mind.

"I will help you, Jared," she said in a low voice.

He looked quickly down at her again, his gray eyes startled and even, very faintly, suspicious. "Madam, I do not understand!"

"I will help you to escape," Bethany repeated. She must not pause to think, to consider her own feelings; she must commit herself quickly, before resolution had time to falter. "You will not accomplish it unaided."

"You would do that?" he said softly, his voice incredulous.

She nodded. He was still looking down at her, and she rose quickly to stand beside him, looking out to sea. She did not dare to meet his eyes in case her own revealed too much.

"Yonder is the only road to freedom," she said quietly, indicating the sparkling, blue-green water. "It is not sufficient to break free of the stockade. You must leave the island altogether. Oh, you could escape from Courtlands easily enough! In fact, you could go now, for you have a horse, and I could do nothing to prevent you, but that would not be freedom, Jared. You would simply have exchanged the life of a slave for that of a hunted animal, and sooner or later you would be recaptured."

"Not alive," he said decisively. "Of that you can be certain. There is, after all, more than one road to freedom."

"No!" The single word came sharp as a cry of pain, and, aware of its betrayal, she bit her lip in dismay. When, after a moment, she spoke again, she did so carefully, for now each word must be considered. "To fling away your life for nothing would be wicked folly. We must wait until there is a ship about to sail, and then somehow you must get aboard just before she puts to sea, so that you are safely away before your flight is discovered."

"Somehow!" he repeated ruefully. "Therein lies the difficulty."

"We shall find a way. We *must* find a way."

There was a pause. Jared was torn between two extremes of emotion. Exultation, because with Bethany's active help an attempted escape might not be quite the forlorn hope he had anticipated; and concern for what might befall her as a result of it. She was still looking towards the sea, her head turned slightly away, and because he was considerably taller than she, the broad brim of her hat hid most of her face from him. All he could see of it was the rounded chin and sweet, determined mouth.

"I ought not to accept such aid from you," he said in a low voice. "You have not paused to consider the consequences."

"They are not worth considering. I may be suspected of helping you, but do you think anyone will venture to accuse me?"

He allowed himself to be convinced of the truth of this. Matthew Court was a man of considerable standing in the colony, a member of the Legislative Assembly and a close personal friend of the Governor. His influence would be more than sufficient to protect his daughter, who, in any case, was unlikely to be thought guilty of anything but a natural feminine compassion which had been exploited by a glib-tongued adventurer.

"Listen to me, Jared." Bethany was looking down now at the whip gripped tightly between her hands, and he could not see her face at all. "I give you my word that I will help you to escape from Barbados, but you must let *me* decide how and when it shall be done. When the time comes, you must not argue with my plans, because in this I have greater knowledge than you of what can or cannot be done. Do you agree?"

"I will agree," he said slowly, "on one condition. That you are placed in no personal danger."

She shrugged. "There will be talk, no doubt, but that is the worst I am likely to suffer, and even then it is probable that I shall be pitied rather than blamed. One thing I *can* promise you. It will be soon. In a little while now I shall be married," her voice faltered for a moment and then steadied again, "and once I have left Courtlands the opportunity to help you will be gone. To help you in any way."

He did not dispute this. The thought of Courtlands without her, without the friendship which alone made his servitude endurable, had been an added spur to his determination to escape. Bethany, and old Gabriel. The only two people in the world who meant anything to him. Now Gabriel was dead, and soon Bethany would be married to that insufferable puppy, Pierce Warren, who had not even the sense to appreciate his rare good fortune.

"I wish I could tell you how grateful I am," he said after a pause, "but that is something which has never come easily to me. I cannot even undertake to repay the debt I owe you."

"Why must you think always in terms of debt and repayment?" There was an edge of bitterness to Bethany's voice. "Can you not accept that a thing may be done freely, for—for friendship's sake?"

"Such friendship has never before been granted to me. Even now I have done nothing to deserve it."

She sighed, the spurt of anger dying as quickly as it had been born. "If we all came by nothing but our just deserts, life would be hard indeed. Come, it is time I returned home."

She walked across to the horses and did not look at him as he helped her to mount. The track through the forest was too narrow for them to ride abreast, and by the time the road was reached she was sufficiently in command of her feelings to behave with outward composure. Presently, when she was alone, she would allow herself to think, which she dare not do while he was still beside her. To think, and to face the situation in which she found herself; which must be faced in secret all her life long, for that life had been mapped out for her years ago, and nothing which had happened had the power to alter it.

Bethany had spoken confidently of Jared making his escape before she herself left Courtlands, but she knew that everything depended on the presence in Bridgetown harbor of a suitable ship. If no ship came . . . ! Yet come it must, because the alternative was too terrible to contemplate.

With her own personal crisis she had managed to come to terms, though only after a period of bitter rebellion against the thing which had befallen her. She loved Jared so deeply that it was a part of her life, a part of her very being, but it was a love which could ask nothing, hope for nothing, except a chance to give him back his freedom. She would marry Pierce

and be a dutiful wife to him, keeping only the memory
of her real love hidden in the secret places of her
heart.

Having once faced the inescapable future, she
tried to put it from her thoughts and to live only for
the present. Time was slipping by so quickly. It was
almost a year since Mr. Warren's death, and once the
period of mourning was over Pierce's impatience
would brook no more delay. She began to grow
reckless, riding with Jared every day and doing
everything she could to discourage Esther from
accompanying them. Usually these rides took them
to the solitude of the forest or the shore, but
sometimes, as when she went dutifully to visit her
great-aunt, it was necessary to pass through the
town, and then there would be curious glances cast at
them, an exchange of significant looks, or a snigger
from a little group of idlers as they passed by.

Bethany, preoccupied with her own problems, was
unaware of this, but Jared noticed it with growing
uneasiness. The poison which Hopson had spread
was doing its deadly work. Free white servants met in
the Bridgetown taverns, and from there talk would be
drifting back to their employers' houses; it could be
only a matter of time before it passed from servant to
master, and so came full circle back to Courtlands
and Matthew Court. Jared said nothing to Bethany,
hoping against hope that he could make his escape
before matters came to a head.

At Courtlands, wedding preparations were again
under way, and in the midst of them, instead of the
serene bride of a year ago, a distraught girl whose
unhappiness found expression in an irritability
wholly foreign to her nature. Friends and servants
puzzled over the change in her, and only Esther
watched her with any degree of comprehension, but
she, with her usual reticence, kept her conclusions to
herself.

The anniversary of Mr. Warren's death came and went, and Bethany, with time growing dangerously short, began to pray for a miracle. She had little hope of the prayer being answered, but one day her father came back from Bridgetown with a guest, whom he introduced as the captain of a Dutch brig which had dropped anchor in the harbor only that day.

Bethany stared incredulously at the visitor. He was a thick-set, ruddy-faced seafarer, but to her he had the appearance of a visitant from Heaven. A Dutch ship was a greater piece of good fortune than she had ever dared to hope for.

"Do you make a long stay here, Captain?" she asked when at length she felt able to say anything at all.

"Perhaps a week, madam, perhaps a little longer," he replied in halting, heavily accented English. "We are in need of repairs, having fallen foul of a Spanish ship of considerably heavier burden than our own."

He went on to describe an incident of a kind familiar enough in the Indies. He had been bound for the Dutch settlement of Curaçao when, some miles south-east of Barbados, the Spanish ship had attacked him. According to the Dutchman, he had been the victim of an unprovoked assault, but Bethany knew well enough that this was one of those piratical affrays which kept relations between Spain and the other nations with colonies in the New World in a constant state of turmoil. Spain's vast power was waning now, but she still looked on the New World as her own special preserve, and resented the presence of any other nationality within its bounds.

Bethany set herself to captivate the Dutchman. By the time he returned to his ship she was in possession of most of the information she needed, and an invitation to him to visit Courtlands again before he sailed had been given and accepted. Next morning, riding with Jared, she told him the good news, and was torn between gladness and pain by the exultant look which swept across his face.

"A Dutch ship, by Heaven!" he exclaimed. "What could be better? Her captain will be less wary than an Englishmen of signing on one whom he is bound to suspect of being a fugitive, especially since I speak his native tongue and can tell him I am myself half Dutch."

"Yet he may still refuse, if he has no need of an extra hand," Bethany pointed out. "I have a better plan. You are much the same height as my father, and I have laid by at home clothes which he wore a few years ago, when he was more spare of flesh than he is now. They should fit you well enough. Dressed thus, and with money to pay for your passage to Curaçao, you will have no need to beg for favors." She saw that he was frowning, and added quickly: "You agreed, remember, that when the time came you would accept my plan without argument."

"I would be an ingrate indeed to argue with such generosity, but there was a condition, too. No danger to yourself."

"This way, there will be none," she replied decisively, "so let us speak no more of that. One thing troubles me. How can you win free of the stockade— for your escape will have to be made at night?"

He shrugged. "Simply enough, if I can come by a coil of rope. It will only be needful to scale the fence."

"The rope you shall have," she said with relief. "I will put all in readiness, then, so that we have only to wait to learn when the ship is to sail." She glanced fleetingly at him, and added with a trace of wistfulness: "It will not be long, Jared. Soon, God aiding us, you will be free."

"And, if I am, it will be due to you alone. Succeed or fail, Miss Court, I shall never forget that."

He leaned across and, before she was aware of his intention, took her hand and lifted it to his lips. With

heightened color she pulled it away, saying breathlessly:

"Do not speak of failure! We must not fail, for the
price would be too high!"

He did not dispute this, for he knew, as well as she,
just what that price would be. He would board the
Dutch ship, or die in the attempt. He would not be
dragged back to the horror and degradation of the
whipping-post and the branding-iron.

The strain of the next few days brought Bethany's
nerves to breaking point, and Pierce, coming to visit
her, found her in a mood which nothing could please.
Once more tempers flared and bitter words were said,
until in fury and dismay he stormed off to find Esther
and pour out his complaints against her sister.

"I do not know what ails her," he concluded
aggrievedly. "In less than a month we are to be wed,
and yet she behaves as though she hates me."

Esther was silent for a moment, and then she said
timidly: "Marriage is a step not lightly taken, Pierce.
So great a change in one's life! You should try to bear
with her."

"I can see that it might be so when bride and groom
are strangers, but, devil take it! Bethany has known
me all her life, and Warrenfield is as familiar to her as
Courtlands itself."

"As a guest, Pierce, not as its mistress. Perhaps
now that the time is near, she is reluctant to leave all
that is familiar to her. Her home, her servants...!"

"Servants?" Pierce's voice sharpened suddenly.
"Or do you mean—one servant? Is it that damned
rebel-convict she is reluctant to part from?"

"Pierce, how can you?" Esther sounded agitated.
"Bethany pities all the slaves, and if she has favored
Vernon above the ordinary—well, it is true that he is
different from the others. Even you must admit that.

Perhaps she is concerned how he will fare when she is
no longer here, but you must not think ...!"

"Don't distress yourself, Esther," Pierce broke in
wearily. "I should not have burdened you with my
troubles, but Bethany drives me to distraction when
she treats me so. Perhaps I had better not come here
again before the wedding."

Bethany, when he informed her stiffly of this
decision, accepted it with a relief which not all her
efforts could entirely disguise. She knew it was
imprudent to treat him so, but there was room in her
mind only for the thought that in a few days' time
Jared would be gone from her. Pierce's presence, and
all that it implied, was more than she could endure.

He returned ill-humoredly to Warrenfield, and a
couple of days later Mr. Court told his daughters that
he had to go north to Speightstown on a matter of
business, and would be absent for several days. That
same afternoon, only a few hours after his departure,
the Dutch sea-captain arrived at Courtlands to
present his compliments and take his leave.

When he found that Mr. Court was absent he
stayed only long enough to take a glass of wine with
the two girls, but that was long enough for Bethany
to discover that the brig would sail on the morning
tide two days hence. She felt at once elated and
despairing, for though everything seemed to be
working in Jared's favor—Mr. Court's absence from
home was an unexpected stroke of good luck—she
was beginning to doubt her own fortitude.

The next day, which, if all went well, was to be
Jared's last day of slavery, was also that on which
Bethany was expected to visit her great-aunt. She
longed to forego the errand, to ride instead to the
privacy of shore or forest, but did not dare to alter her
usual custom in case suspicion was aroused.

So to Bridgetown they went, occupying the journey
by completing their plans, and somehow she

managed to remain outwardly calm and practical in spite of the tight knot of misery within her. When they reached Mrs. Milford's house, she was astonished, and even a little alarmed, to find that the old lady had come to the door to greet her. Great-Aunt Elizabeth so seldom bestirred herself to any activity that such a departure from normal was disquieting. Jared lifted Bethany from her horse and was about to lead the animals away when Mrs. Milford's sharp voice detained him.

"One moment, young man!" As he turned, she beckoned imperiously. "Come here!"

He came slowly to the foot of the shallow steps leading to the door, and looked inquiringly at her. Bethany, uneasy without quite knowing why, had halted midway between them.

The old lady's shrewd, bright eyes, sunken in the heavy, fleshy face, studied Jared from head to foot, noting, it seemed, every detail of his appearance. She said curtly: "Your name?"

"Jared Vernon, madam." He bowed. "To serve you."

"H'm!" For a moment or two longer she regarded him, and then made a gesture of dismissal. "You may go! Bethany, come within!"

She made her ponderous way into the house, Bethany following with growing uneasiness. Mrs. Milford lowered her bulk laboriously into her favorite chair, heaved a sigh of relief, and then said in a tone of the utmost exasperation:

"So gossip speaks truth for once! Upon my soul, Bethany Court, I never thought you could be such a fool!"

Bethany stared. "Madam, I do not understand."

"Don't try to play the innocent with me, my girl! The whole of Bridgetown is sniggering over tales about you and that groom of yours. I would have heard 'em myself, long since, had I been in the habit

of receiving visitors. Yes, you may well blush! It was
only yesterday I learned what you have been up to!
Mary Steed was here—Mary Steed, who hasn't set
foot in this house these five years—sympathizing
with me and assuring me she didn't believe a word of
the scandal. Believe it? I'll warrant she had a hand in
starting it!"

She paused at last for breath, and Bethany, whose
bewilderment had rapidly given place to indignation,
said angrily: "This is quite absurd! Surely, Great-
Aunt, *you* do not believe such malicious gossip?"

"I didn't," Mrs. Milford replied frankly, "until I
took a look at the young spark for myself. Well, you
are not the first woman to lose her head over a
handsome serving-man!" She flung out an accusing
finger as Bethany made a little gesture of protest.
"That is all he is, in spite of his fine manners and
lordly bearing! A servant! One of your father's slaves,
bought and paid for. Upon my soul! I would expect a
Court to have more pride."

"And I would expect you, madam, to be less ready
to believe ill of a member of your own family."

"Had I less knowledge of the world, miss, I might
have more charity," Mrs. Milford replied tartly. "I
told your father, when your poor mother died, that he
should get both you girls married as soon as you were
fifteen, before you had any opportunity for mischief,
but he would pay no need. And then to let you have a
servant the like of that one! As well throw you
straight into the fellow's arms!" She paused, and
again the admonishing finger was lifted. "There will
be an end to it, Bethany, do you hear me? You will
send the young man back to the plantation immediately. He is not to attend you again after today!"

Bethany turned abruptly away to the window and
stood there staring out, her anger, dismay and shame
all perishing in an overwhelming flood of anguish.
What did it matter? What could anything matter

after tonight, when Jared would have gone either to
freedom, or to his death?

"Yes," she said, half to herself, "there will be an
end to it. He will never ride with me again, after
today."

Bethany stood at the window of her bedchamber,
watching for a movement in the moonlit garden
which would tell her that Jared had accomplished the
first part of his escape. For the hundredth time she
reviewed in her mind the preparations she had made,
fearful, even at this late stage, that something vital
had been forgotten.

The rope which he needed to scale the fence had
been smuggled into his hut several days before, and if
he could surmount that obstacle he would have little
to fear at the stockade, for once the gates were locked
for the night no guard was kept. Where, after all, was
a runaway slave to go if he broke out of his quarters?
The sea was a sure barrier on every side.

Once free of the stockade, Jared must make his
way along the edge of the plantation and through the
stableyard and garden to the door where she would
meet him. The clothes and a sword she had concealed
in a room close by, the gold was in a purse beneath
her pillow. Once disguised, he would have to cross the
garden again to reach the road; a half-hour's walk
would bring him to the town and so, God willing, to
the safety of the Dutch ship.

In the garden below, a tall figure emerged
cautiously from the shelter of a clump of trees, stood
for a few seconds looking towards the house, and
then withdrew again into the shadows. Bethany
picked up the candle she had left burning, showed the
light briefly at the window, and then tiptoed across to
the door between her room and the adjoining one,
where Esther slept.

With infinite care she opened it a crack and stood listening, hearing with relief her sister's deep, even breathing. Esther was a poor sleeper, and Bethany's greatest dread had been that the other girl would hear her moving about and come to investigate. For that reason she had not dared to remain fully dressed, since that would immediately have aroused Esther's suspicions, and she was clad now in her night-gown of ivory-colored satin, her hair loose about her shoulders.

Esther had not even stirred in her sleep. Bethany silently closed the door, fetched the purse of gold and slipped quietly from the room.

She stole along the corridor and down the stairs, her soft slippers soundless on the polished hardwood floor, one hand holding up her trailing robe. The bolts slid silently back—she had already assured herself that they would make no sound—and as soon as the door swung open Jared slipped softly in. He replied reassuringly to her anxious, whispered question, and she pointed to the door of a room a few yards away.

"The clothes are in the chest below the window. Make haste! I will keep watch here."

He took the candle she held out to him and disappeared into the room. Bethany stood motionless, listening intently, but no sound reached her straining ears from the sleep-wrapped house, while from the garden, beyond the outer door which yet stood ajar, came only the ordinary small noises of the night. She went softly forward and pulled the door wide, and moonlight flooded in as bright as day. Above the dark shapes of trees the sky was brilliant with stars, and below, fireflies like smaller, nearer stars danced among the leaves.

At last a faint sound made her turn and Jared was coming towards her, a stranger now in dark blue satin laced with gold, with lace at throat and wrist, and a long rapier slung from an embroidered baldrick. The plumbed hat was in his hand, and his long, dark hair, falling thickly across his shoulders, took the place of the fashionable periwig. He halted before her, where she stood with her back against the open door, and for a few moments they looked at one another without speaking. He had left the candle in the room, but the moonlight was bright enough for them to see each other clearly.

"Take this!" Bethany held out the heavy purse. "It will buy your passage to Curaçao, with perhaps a little to spare." He took it with some reluctance, and she added quickly: "And if we are to part in friendship, Jared, do not dare to speak of repaying me."

She had tried to speak lightly, but her voice shook uncontrollably and she broke off, biting her lip. She had vowed to herself that she would be strong, that she would bid him farewell without betraying herself, but now that the moment of parting had come, resolution was not proof against the utter desolation she felt. She could only gaze helplessly up at him, her face white and defenseless in the uncaring moonlight.

"Bethany!" Jared's low voice was rough with emotion. "Bethany!"

She was not aware of having moved, could never afterwards be sure which of them had been the first to do so, but next moment she was in his arms, and everything else was forgotten.

Forgotten by them both. In that impetuous, instinctive coming together they were conscious only of their need of each other, a need which could no longer be denied. For Jared, even the freedom now so tantalizingly close had for the moment ceased to beckon, and Bethany, with his kisses on her lips, her face, her throat, was lost and drowning in delight.

Was it a sound, a movement, or simply the sense of another, alien presence which pierced that brief rapture? She would never know, but she opened her eyes and looked past Jared's shoulder to see, a dozen paces away in the mouth of a nearby path, the head overseer, with Will Hopson beside him.

They stood and stared, with slack jaws and starting eyes, and in Becket's face, at least, consternation was plainly written. For an instant of frozen horror Bethany stared back, incapable even of thought, and then her mind cleared and with a flash of inspiration she saw what must be done. As Jared, becoming aware of her sudden tenseness, lifted his head, she clasped him even closer and whispered urgently, her lips against his cheek:

"Go into the house, and for the love of God, do not turn your head!"

The desperation in her voice warned him to obey without question, and as he stepped past her into the shielding darkness Bethany moved a pace or two towards the staring men and demanded, in a low voice unsteady with what might well have been anger:

"What is the meaning of this intrusion?"

It was Becket who answered, apologetically yet in the tone of one who had sought only to do his duty. "Miss Court, we were returning from the town when we thought we saw a man near the edge of the plantation, coming towards the house. We feared he might be seeking to break in, so, knowing the master is from home, we followed. We lost sight of the man, and have been searching the garden in case he was hiding there."

"And no doubt it is because my father *is* from home that you have been carousing in the Bridgetown taverns until this hour," Bethany said coldly. "With the result that you see robbers behind every bush. You had better go back to your quarters and sleep some sense into your fuddled wits."

"With respect, Miss Court," Hopson put in slyly,

"there must have been *someone* lurking here to rouse you and bring you down. The same intruder as we saw, I'll warrant!"

She looked at him with anger and disgust. There was a knowing smirk on his heavy face, and his glance roamed over her with an insolence which made her acutely conscious of her night-gown and her unbound hair. She drew herself up, pulling the gown close again about her throat, and said in a deliberately meaning tone:

"You were mistaken. You saw no one. Do you understand me?"

Becket assured her hastily that they did. He was acutely uncomfortable. He had acted in good faith, but had he known he was to find his master's daughter in the arms of an unknown gentleman whom she was obviously admitting surreptitiously to the house, no power on earth would have brought him into the garden that night. He was only too anxious to forget what he had seen, and endeavored, discreetly, to tell her so.

She cut him short, and looked at Will Hopson. It was there, she knew, that the real danger lay. He grinned impudently back at her.

"To be sure, we were mistaken! There be none here but us, and never was. We understand, mistress!"

Becket gripped him by the arm and with a muttered apology thrust him away along the path, but as they went Bethany heard Hopson say something to his companion, and then laugh in a way which made her cheeks burn with shame. By tomorrow, she knew, the tale would be on everyone's lips, but she could take comfort, at least, from the certainty that at present neither Hopson nor Becket had any suspicion of her companion's real identity.

When they had passed from sight, she turned and went back into the house where Jared stood watching and listening. She was trembling violently now, and when he put his arms about her she leaned weakly against him, but by this time sanity had returned to them both. Whatever wild dreams and desires had for a moment possessed them were impossible of fulfillment, and they had no choice but to say farewell.

"They have gone," she said in a shaken whisper. "In a few minutes it will be safe for you to go also."

"Leaving you to face the consequences alone? Hopson will not keep silent about what he saw just now, and when it is learned that I have escaped, it will be known also that you aided me."

"That will not matter, as long as you are by then safely beyond danger of recapture. As for Hopson, there is no way to prevent him from talking. Even if you were to go back to the stockade it would make no difference."

"And when your father hears the story? When young Warren hears it?"

"They will not believe it. I can convince them that it is untrue." Bethany spoke with more confidence than she felt, aware only of the pressing need to allay any anxiety he felt on her behalf. She put her hands on his shoulders and looked earnestly into his face. "I can face gossip, as long as I know that it is not in vain. As long as I know that you are free. That is the only thing that matters to me." Her voice broke, and the next words were almost inaudible. "Jared, go now—and God go with you!"

He could find nothing to say. He took her face gently between his hands and kissed her with lingering tenderness, tasting her tears salt against his lips. Then he turned silently from her, stepping from the house to vanish without a backward glance into the shadows of the garden. For a long while Bethany stood there, anxiously listening, but all remained quiet, and at last she closed the door and went wearily to her room, to keep the vigil which

would not end until she was certain that he was
safely at sea.

Two days later, Pierce Warren flung himself from
a lathered horse at the door of Courtlands, thrust
aside the Negro slave who admitted him and stormed
into the house, demanding to see Bethany. The
frightened servant began to stammer something
which might have been either excuse or explanation,
and then a door opened nearby and Esther appeared
on the threshold, staring in wide-eyed dismay. Pierce
strode across to her.

"Where is Bethany? I want to see her! At once!"

"You cannot! At least, not at once!" Esther seemed
so agitated that she was almost incoherent. "Pierce, I
beg of you ... !"

He glanced over his shoulder at the gaping
servant, and then thrust her into the room again and
followed, shutting the door behind him. He was white
with temper, with a rigid look about his mouth.

"I insist on seeing her! I want to know why these
damned lying tales have been spread concerning her
and Vernon. It seems that all Bridgetown is either
laughing at me or pitying me."

"How did you find out?" Esther stammered. "Who
told you? We thought ... !"

"You thought you could keep it from me? No,
Esther, there is always some good friend who feels it
his duty to open one's eyes. I suppose I should be
grateful for that!"

"Perhaps what you heard was exaggerated,"
Esther suggested desperately. "Gossip always is!"

"I will tell you what I heard," Pierce replied grimly.
"I heard that Vernon was her lover, and that she has
shamelessly flaunted the fact before the whole town.
That the other night two of your overseers surprised

her in his arms, though they were not then aware of
his identity since Bethany had furnished him with a
disguise and the means to break free of his bondage.
That she was even then bidding him farewell." He
went past her into the room and slammed gloves and
riding-whip on to the table with a viciousness which
was a sufficient indication of his mood. "Fine tales,
by God, for a man to hear of his promised wife less
than a month before their wedding!"

Esther was still standing just inside the door,
biting her lip and twisting her hands together in
obvious indecision. He looked impatiently across at
her.

"Will you fetch her, or must I? For see her I will,
whether she wishes it or not." He waited a moment,
but she did not speak. "So be it! Where is she?"

"She is in her room." Esther stepped quickly in
front of him as he moved again towards the door.
"Father has forbidden her to leave it without his
permission. He returned from Speightstown last
night. Great Aunt-Elizabeth sent for him. Pierce, I
have never seen him so angry! Not with Bethany!"

He had put out his hand to move her aside, but at
that he checked, staring at her in a stunned fashion.
"You do not mean it is true?"

"That she helped Vernon to escape?" Esther
nodded. "Yes, that is true. Father has gone now to see
His Excellency, to convince him, if he can, that she
did not realize the gravity of what she was doing."

That brought Pierce up short, showing him an
aspect of the affair which, possessed by jealous fury,
he had not previously considered. Jared Vernon was
no common felon, transported for some trifling
offense. He was a rebel, convicted of high treason,
and in England there were appallingly harsh
penalties for aiding such as he. Yet this was not
England, and Matthew Court was a man of wealth

and influence; it was inconceivable that the Law might be set in motion against his daughter.

"My God! How could she be such a fool?" he said despairingly. "Surely she knew what the consequences might be?"

"I do not think she cared," Esther replied in a low voice. "You know she has always maintained that the rebels sold into slavery were unjustly used."

There was a pause. Pierce stood with bent head, drumming his fingers on the table, his thoughts for the moment dominated by alarm on Bethany's behalf. Esther walked slowly across to the window and stood looking out, as though not knowing what else to say.

After a little while, she saw her father ride up to the door. A groom came running to take his horse, and Mr. Court passed from sight as he entered the house. They heard him speaking to a servant in the hall, and then he came slowly into the room; his face was drawn and haggard, and he looked at least ten years older.

Pierce lifted his head as he entered, but made no move to greet him. Mr. Court lookd at him, and lifted his hands in a helpless gesture.

"Pierce!" he said heavily. "What can I say?"

"Father!" Esther spoke with breathless anxiety. "What is going to happen? Is Bethany in any danger?"

"There is nothing to fear, my child," Mr. Court replied kindly. "For that, at least, we must be thankful." He raised his hand to check the questions she seemed about to ask. "You shall know everything directly. I have sent for your sister."

Pierce spoke for the first time. "By what means *did* Vernon make his escape?"

Mr. Court frowned. "Has Esther not told you? Bethany gave him money, and clothes of mine so that he would not be known for a runaway slave, and he had the impudence to take passage aboard the Dutch brig which has been lying in the harbor. Had I been here when his flight was discovered I might have succeeded in keeping secret Bethany's part in the affair, but as it is ... !"

"Might you have done so, sir?" There was a note of savage skepticism in Pierce's voice. "Even though your own servants saw her that night in Vernon's arms?"

"One of those servants bore both Bethany and Vernon a grudge," Mr. Court reminded him sternly. "Are we to condemn her on his word alone?"

"Are we to believe rather that both this man and his companion are lying? That they would dare to invent such a tale about your daughter out of sheer malice? Unlikely, to say the least! And if they are speaking truth, it follows that all the rest must be true also."

"Yes, it is true!" It was Esther who spoke, in a high, unnatural voice utterly unlike her normal tone. "I can keep silent no longer! It is only just that you should know the truth about her."

The two men swung round to confront her as though jerked by the same invisible cord, staring at her in the most complete astonishment. She had taken a pace forward and now faced them with mingled apprehension and defiance, her hands tightly clenched, her chin up and a spot of color burning in either cheek.

"I had suspected it for a long time," she went on fiercely, "for they rode so often to lonely places in the forest or along the shore, and Bethany was always angry if I went with them. Then the night before last, some sound awakened me. We were alone in the house except for the servants, and I was frightened. I went to rouse Bethany, but the door between our rooms was locked. I was just going to call out to her when I heard...!" She broke off, making a little gesture of embarrassment and distaste. "Oh, I cannot tell you! But Vernon was there with her, in her bedchamber."

There was a moment of complete and utter silence, a moment so charged with emotion that the air itself seemed to tremble with it. Pierce was the first to speak.

"My God!" he said bitterly. "These past months she would scarcely let me touch her, yet all the while a filthy slave...!"

He broke off abruptly, and turned sharply away to stand by the table, his head bent and his hands gripped hard on the edge of the polished wood. Mr. Court said hoarsely:

"Why did you not tell me this before?"

Esther moved her hands helplessly. "I did not know *what* to do. I spent the rest of that night trying to decide whether my duty was to speak, or to keep silent. Then in the morning we had word that Vernon had escaped, and it seemed that the decision had been made for me. He had gone, and Bethany would forget him, and perhaps it would be best for everyone if I kept the secret of her shame. Then Hopson told what he and Becket saw that night, and now everyone knows...!"

"Everyone knows her for the wanton she is!" Pierce broke in harshly. "Your loyalty to your sister does you credit, Esther, but she is not worthy of it."

There was a pause. Mr. Court sat down and took his head between his hands; Pierce remained standing bowed above the table. Neither was looking at Esther, and for a second or two her glance flickered from one to the other with sly, malicious satisfaction. Then a light footstep sounded outside the door, and in an instant she had schooled her expression once more to one of demure regret.

Bethany came into the room. She was very pale,

with dark shadows beneath her eyes, but she entered with quiet dignity, giving no sign of whatever alarm or humiliation she felt. Apparently she had been told that Pierce was there, for she betrayed no surprise at his presence. He had raised his head to look at her, and for a few seconds she looked steadily back, facing the contempt and condemnation in his eyes. Only when her glance turned to her father's hunched figure did anxiety creep into it. She said uncertaintly:

"You sent for me, sir?"

Slowly, almost unwillingly, he lifted his head, and she flinched with shock at what she saw in his eyes. He rose to his feet, saying, in a voice as cold as his look:

"To tell you that you may consider yourself fortunate. His Excellency is prepare to accept that you are no more than a silly, gullible girl made use of by a plausible rogue. As far as the Law is concerned, you have nothing to fear."

"His Excellency is generous," she replied in a low voice. "I am well aware that I could be held guilty of a criminal act, even though I had no wish to offend against the Law, and still do not feel that I have done so."

"But though the Law will inflict no punishment upon you," her father went on in a hard voice, "the world in general is less forbearing. You have not only brought shame and ruin upon yourself, but also disgrace upon our family, and upon our good friends, the Warrens, and for that I cannot forgive you." He turned to Pierce. "You know the truth now, and your wedding is but a month away. You, more than anyone, have the right to pass judgment."

Pierce was staring at Bethany, as he had been staring from the moment she entered the room, hating her because, in spite of everything, her beauty still gave her a measure of power over him. Esther's words burned in his mind. "I had suspected it for a long time... Vernon was with her in her bedchamber." Bethany had betrayed him, given herself to that arrogant rebel-slave with the mocking eyes, and made of her future husband an object of ridicule and pity. He wanted to hurt her, to shatter her composure and make her suffer for the suffering she had inflicted upon him.

"There will be no wedding," he said cruelly. "You cannot in honor, Mr. Court, hold me to a marriage contract with a proven whore."

He had the satisfaction of knowing that he had stung her, for her head jerked up and color flamed across her white face. After one, stunned, disbelieving look at him she turned impetuously to her father, but though his face was ashen, he made not the slightest response to that unspoken appeal.

"I cannot hold you to it, Pierce. I can only remind you that this union between our families was planned long ago, and was your father's earnest wish as well as mine."

Pierce hesitated. He, too, had earnestly desired the marriage, with all that it meant of increased wealth and influence; on that score, he desired it still. There was no marriageable girl in Barbados whose dowry matched Bethany Court's. Except one. He drew a deep breath.

"It is a union, sir, which I have no wish to forego," he said deliberately. "You have another daughter, whose virtue is beyond question. Will you give *her* to me in marriage instead?"

For several seconds no one spoke. Esther, who had sunk into a chair by the table and covered her eyes with her hand, looked up quickly, the color flooding into her pale cheeks; Bethany drew a sharp, audible breath; and Mr. Court stood staring at Pierce as though not quite understanding what he had said.

"You are asking to marry Esther instead of her sister?" he said slowly at length.

"If she will have me!" Pierce, too, was pale, but he spoke with firm resolution. "Will you, Esther?"

·She made a frightened, helpless movement with her hands and looked imploringly at her father. He was recovering now from his astonishment, and after a little thought said gravely:

"If Esther is willing, Pierce, I have no objection to such an arrangement, but I would not have either of you act too hastily. It is a step impossible to retrace."

"I do not wish to draw back, sir, now or ever," Pierce replied steadily, "and if Esther marries me, I swear she will never have cause to regret it."

"Esther?" Mr. Court looked dubiously at his daughter, sitting now with her hands gripped tightly together in her lap, and her eyes downcast. "Have you nothing to say?"

"Only that if you and Pierce wish it, sir, I will marry him," she replied timidly, without looking up, "and that I will do my best to be a good and dutiful wife."

Bethany could endure no more. She ran from the room, and presently, without having the least recollection of coming there, found herself once more in her own room. Sinking down on the carved chest at the foot of the bed, she sat staring blankly before her, still numb with shock at what had happened. "I can face gossip," she had told Jared, but she had believed then that she would be facing it as Mrs. Pierce Warren of Warrenfield; that no matter how shocked and angry and suspicious Pierce and her father might be at first, they would believe her when she swore to them that there had been nothing between her and Jared save that one embrace.

Yet she had been given no opportunity to tell them that; no opportunity to tell them anything at all. They had judged and condemned her without giving her a chance to utter one word in her own defense, accepting without question the implications of the tale Will Hopson had so gleefully related. She had read that in their eyes as soon as she faced them, and though she had forced herself to give no sign she had felt as though solid ground was suddenly crumbling away beneath her feet. They believed her guilty, and when it was seen that her long-standing betrothal had been set aside, that it was Esther, and not she, who was to be Pierce's bride, what hope had she that anyone else would believe her innocent?

Yet why? Why had they been so ready to condemn her on the word of a vindictive servant? Bethany felt sure that her father's anger, when he first returned from Speightstown, had been caused almost entirely by anxiety at the danger in which she had placed herself by abetting the escape of a convicted rebel. That anxiety was not allayed, but he, as well as Pierce, was convinced that Jared had been her lover. Something had happened to give them what they considered to be unquestionable proof of that; but what?

For hours she wrestled with the problem. Her maid came to summon her to supper, but she refused to leave the sanctuary of her room; Tabitha, looking at her with loving anxiety, brought food and drink on a tray, but she left it untouched. A suspicion had forced itself into her mind, a suspicion so ugly and frightening that she kept trying to thrust it from her thoughts, to believe that it had never occurred to her at all.

At last, long after darkness had fallen, she faced the fact that she would know no peace until she had put the hateful suspicion to the test. She could hear Esther moving about in the adjoining room, and reluctantly, because she was so fearful of what she might discover, Bethany went through the connecting door into her sister's bedchamber.

Esther was sitting on the stool before the dressing-table, gazing dreamily into the silver-framed mirror and so engrossed in her own thoughts that she never heard the door open. Only when Bethany moved forward and met her sister's glance in the mirror did Esther become aware of her presence. She uttered a little cry and swung round to face her.

"Bethany! Oh, what a fright you gave me, stealing up behind me like that!"

Bethany did not immediately reply. She was looking at her sister, studying the familiar countenance as though it were that of a stranger, as though she were seeing it for the first time in her life. Trying to reach beyond the outward diffidence, the gentleness and timidity, and to judge whether there was a hardness and a selfishness there which no one had ever suspected.

"Esther," she said bluntly at last, "what have you been saying about me to Father and to Pierce?"

It was a shot in the dark, but it struck home more surely even than she had expected. Esther shrank back, every trace of color draining from her face, and looked up at Bethany with wide, terrified eyes.

"How did you find out?" she whispered.

"I did not." Bethany, sick and shaken at finding her suspicion confirmed, spoke with difficulty. "I could only guess. They would not have believed such things of me on the servants' word alone. Someone else had convinced them—someone they thought they could trust. It could only be you." Her voice broke, in spite of all her efforts to keep it steady. "Esther, why? How could you do such a thing?"

"You really do not know, do you?" Esther was still pale, but now anger was making her defiant. "You thought that everything could go on as before! That nothing could ever make Father think ill of you, and that you only had to smile at Pierce and assure him that you were innocent, and he would marry you and so give the lie to this scandal you have stirred up. That Bethany Court could do just as she pleased and never have to face the consequences. Well, you were wrong! I have made sure of that! I told them I knew that Vernon was with you in your room the other night."

Bethany moved shakily to the bed and sat down on the edge of it, for she was trembling so much that she was incapable of remaining on her feet. The vindictiveness in Esther's voice, the malicious triumph in her eyes, had a nightmare quality, as though some alien spirit had taken possession of her.

"That is a lie!" she whispered.

"Yes!" Esther made the admission with no hint of shame. "But even if you tell them so, they will not believe you, since he was seen leaving the house. It is my word against yours, and which of us has the more reason to lie?"

Bethany recognized the truth of this. Anyone else might be doubted, but not Esther, for who would believe that gentle, timid creature capable of lying about so grave a matter as her sister's honor? This vindictive stranger with her hard, contemptuous eyes was an Esther which no one had ever known existed; that Bethany herself would not have credited before tonight.

"Tell me one thing," she said in a low voice. "Do you really believe that Jared was my lover?"

Esther shrugged. "Does it matter what I believe?"

"Of course it matters! If you honestly believe that I have betrayed Pierce, there is some reason for what you did. Some reason other than malice."

"What difference does it make?" Esther's voice trembled with the intensity of her feelings. "Perhaps Vernon was not your lover—I do not know—but you wanted him to be. Do you think I could not tell that? You were false to Pierce a score of times in thought, if not in deed, and the one is as vile a betrayal as the other. You deserve to be punished! I did not plan what happened today, but when the chance offered I took it without hesitation or regret."

Bethany tried to protest, but she was given no chance. It seemed that now Esther had started to speak, nothing could stop her, and the pent-up bitterness and resentment of a lifetime came pouring out. To Bethany, stunned and horrified by that flood of malice, the words seemed to fill the room like a flock of birds; small, fierce birds with beating wings and sharp, wounding beaks.

"I never guessed that he would ask to marry me instead, but I will make him a good wife. Better than you would ever have done, for you care nothing for him and I have loved him ever since I can remember. But he never had eyes for anyone but you. No one had! Bethany Court, so beautiful and capable and clever! Admired and praised by everyone! Father—and Mother, too—could see no fault in you, while for me there was only a sort of kindly impatience. Bethany Court's sister! How I have hated being known thus! How I have hated you!" She sprang to her feet and came to stand directly in front of Bethany, studying her with eyes blazing with satisfaction. Her voice, her whole figure, seemed to vibrate with triumph. "Now all that is ended. You are disgraced, ruined—and for what? For the sake of a man concerned only to contrive his escape from bondage, an adventurer who used you for his own ends, and no doubt despised you even as he did so."

With a tremendous effort Bethany roused herself from her state of shocked numbness. She rose to her feet and confronted Esther proudly.

"Even if that were true," she said quietly, "I would still count it all worth while, for he is free. Freedom meant more to him than life, and so I have given him both life and freedom. Beside that, everything else is of no account. If you cannot understand that, Esther, then, for all your talk of loving Pierce, you understand nothing at all.".

She stepped past the other girl, and steadily, without looking back, went through to her own room and closed the door behind her, turning the key in the lock. Only then, alone and with no need to dissemble, did she allow herself to give way, sinking into her former seat on the chest and hugging herself with both arms as though mortally cold.

"How I have hated you," Esther had said, and proof of those incredible words had been blazing out of her eyes and throbbing in her voice. Esther! Her sister, her twin, the other part of herself. Nursing that hatred all these years, burying it so deep that no one ever suspected its existence; as she would bury it again tomorrow and be again the timid, diffident Esther everyone knew. Meek and dutiful, slipping quietly into the place which should have been Bethany's, and, by doing so, proclaiming to all the world that the scandalous stories concerning her sister were true.

Bethany shivered, contemplating, with dread and despair, the humiliations in store for her. Yet Jared was free, so what matter that the price she had to pay for his freedom were greater than either of them could have foreseen. He was free! She spoke the words aloud, making of them a talisman against the future, a prop to her failing courage. It was the only comfort she was to have for many lonely, difficult months.

Five

Bethany, huddled in the stern of the longboat, was dreaming, tormented in nightmare not merely by the lately endured terrors of storm and shipwreck, but by fragments of memory of the two endless years which had passed since her life crumbled into ruins about her. Of her father, stern and withdrawn, unforgiving in his bitter disillusion; of Esther, demure on her marriage-day; radiant with her infant son in her arms; of Great-Aunt Elizabeth's testy voice: "Send Bethany to Jamaica, Matthew, to Cousin Stanton. You will never find the slut a husband here." Barbados fading like a cloud on the horizon; the unseasonable storm of hurricane violence shrieking out of the darkness to batter a stout ship into a foundering hulk; Matilda, Bethany's quadroon maid, screaming high and shrill in panic until a great wave swept her helplessly away, her cries lost in the howling of the wind.

When Bethany awoke, it was to reality only a little

less frightening than her dreams. She was lying on the bottom of the boat, huddled on the wet boards with her head pillowed on her arm. The sailors had rigged a piece of canvas to cover her, shielding her from the spray, and from the rays of the sun now high in the clearing sky, but the taste of the sea was still in her mouth, and its salt crusted her parched lips. Painfully she dragged herself up, each movement sending stabs of agony through her cramped limbs, and crept out from beneath the meager shelter.

The scene which greeted her was anything but reassuring. Though the storm had passed, a heavy sea was still running; great waves, blue-green and streaked with foam, which at one moment lifted the tiny craft to dizzy crests, and the next plunged it headlong into the chasm between. A sea which stretched empty to the horizon on every hand, devoid of any other sign of life.

There were half a dozen sailors in the boat, including John Pendlecombe, the bo'sun, who was at the tiller, while two of the men bent to the oars. Bethany, emerging from her shelter, found herself close beside him. As the boat lifted again she cast another desperate glance all around, and then looked fearfully at Pendlecombe.

"The others?" she whispered huskily.

He shook his head. "No trace of 'em, mistress," he said grimly. "Even if they survived, we've been drove far apart. 'Tis a miracle we be still afloat ourselves."

Bethany shuddered. A fine ship, and all those lives, devoured by the waves, swallowed up by the greedy waters as though they had never been. Captain Mitchell was a friend of her father's, and Bethany had known the big, bluff seafarer all her life; it was natural that she should have been put into his care for the short voyage to Jamaica. Now Mitchell was dead, and what was to become of her and these other few survivors of the disaster? She was afraid to put the question into words.

She passed her tongue across her dry lips. "Is there any fresh water?"

"Aye!" the bo'sun called an order to the men in the bows, and one of them drew water from a cask—a pitifully small cask, Bethany saw with dismay—and bore it carefully to her.

She sipped it slowly, making it last as long as she could, and smiled uncertainly at the man as she returned the empty mug. He, and the other men, were almost strangers to her, their faces only vaguely familiar from seeing them as they went about their duties during the past two days, and she did not know whether it would be wiser to treat them in friendly fashion or to hold herself aloof.

"Best get beneath the canvas again, mistress!" Pendlecombe, a grizzled, leathern-faced man with a broad West Country accent, spoke with rough kindliness. "Sun and wind be mighty fierce on delicate skin."

Bethany recognized the wisdom of the advice, for already she could feel the fierce heat burning her face and throat and bare shoulders. Her fashionable, low-cut gown of amber silk, the filmy lace which should have veiled the top of the bodice reduced to a stringy rag, gave no protection, and she had not so much as a handkerchief with which to cover herself. Conscious suddenly of the men's eyes upon her, she crept again into the patch of shadow beneath the sailcloth.

There, hidden from her companions, she gave way to the fears which beset her, weeping quietly with her head buried in the crook of her arm. They might be picked up, or make landfall, or they might drift until death claimed them, but whatever befell was likely to mean days penned in the cramped confines of the tiny boat with these rough sailors, with no privacy but that provided by the flimsy canvas shelter.

The heat beneath it was stifling now, and at length she sank again into a stupor which was half sleep and half unconsciousness, but still haunted by evil dreams. When at last she jerked awake once more, she could not at first remember where she was, and when she did, found it difficult to comprehend the sound which had roused her. The sailors were shouting in jubilation.

Bethany struggled to hands and knees and crawled out into the open. The boat lay deep in the trough between two waves and at first she could see nothing but the green, surging water rising on every hand. Then they were tossed aloft again, and she caught a glimpse of a great ship bearing towards them a quarter of a mile away.

For a few seconds only the boat poised dizzily on the wave's crest before plunging down again, but in those seconds the whole scene imprinted itself like a picture in Bethany's mind. The ship, her arched sails white above stately, gilded hull, dipping towards them across the glimmering sea, against a clear, pale sky which heralded the approach of nightfull. A blessed sight, the most welcome sight in the whole world. Bethany closed her eyes for a moment and whispered a prayer of heartfelt gratitude.

"A Spaniard, by the build of her," she heard John Pendlecombe remark, and glanced at him in quick dismay. He noticed this, and added reassuringly: "No need to fret, mistress! The Dons have little kindness for other nations, but they'll not offer harm to a lady o' your quality."

Bethany hoped that he was right. She had heard horrific tales of the fate of women who fell into Spanish hands; it was as bad, almost, as being captured by pirates. Her first rush of relief tempered now by misgiving, she scanned the approaching vessel anxiously at each opportunity. The ship flew no flag, but when she drew close enough for those in the boat to make out the name inscribed amid the gilded carving on her bows, it brought little reassurance, for the name was *Santa Maria.*

Yet in spite of this, and the typically Spanish lines of the hull with its towering poop, the voice which presently hailed them from the ship was as English as their own. Bethany cast a bewildered glance at the bo'sun, and saw that although he answered the shout he looked more perturbed than relieved.

In that sea it was no easy task to bring the boat in close to the ship's side, but it was accomplished at last. A rope-ladder came snaking down, and then, when those above saw that there was a woman in the boat, they lowered also a wicker contraption like a gigantic basket so that she could be hauled on deck.

With the help of sailors Bethany scrambled in, but it was a perilous undertaking in that tossing boat, and she was drenched again before the basket lifted above the reach of the waves. She crouched with tight-shut eyes, half paralyzed with terror, as the frail vehicle jerked slowly upwards, swinging to and fro and bumping against the ship's side. After what seemed an eternity it swung safely across the bulwarks and was lowered to the deck, where it rolled gently over on to its side, spilling her out anyhow.

Wet and bedraggled, shivering a little in the cool breeze which had sprung up as evening approached, she scrambled to her feet and looked apprehensively about her, aware as she did so of a stir of surprise and gratification among the men who had gathered curiously to watch the castaways come aboard. They were certainly not Spaniards, but they were as motley a crowd as she had ever seen, the only note of uniformity being struck by the murderous array of weapons each one carried. Their attire ranged from filthy, rawhide breeches to the laced coat and plumed hat of a man who stood in the forefront of the throng, and it was upon this man that Bethany's horrified and fascinated gaze became riveted.

He was the ugliest individual she had ever seen. Of medium height, with tremendously broad shoulders, and long arms which hung almost to his knees, he resembled nothing so much as some gigantic ape tricked out in human guise, a resemblance heightened by the heavy jaw and shallow brow and small, close-set dark eyes. Greasy black curls flowed across his shoulders, and, where coat and shirt gaped open to the waist, his huge chest showed matted with black hair as thick as an animal's. He took a step towards her and she shrank back in horror, yet when he spoke his voice, though harsh and loud, held an incongruous note of genuine refinement.

"By the devil himself, here's a fair prize to be washed up by the sea! Welcome aboard the *Santa Maria*, madam. I am Captain Lucas Roach, master of this vessel."

Before she could make any reply, John Pendlecombe appeared at the top of the rope ladder. He jumped down on to the deck and came quickly to Bethany's side.

"You'll treat the lady wi' due respect," he said belligerently. "She be English, like yourself, and daughter to a rich gentleman o' Barbados."

Captain Roach looked at him. The smile with which he had greeted Bethany was still on his wide, thin mouth, but there was an expression in his eyes which sent Pendlecombe's hand groping uneasily towards the knife at his belt.

"She can be daughter to the Devil himself for all I care," Roach said softly, "but if you seek to give *me* orders, my friend, I'll toss you back whence you came and let you shift for yourself. Master I am, and master I'll stay."

"Master of a crew o' cut-throats," the bo'sun retorted. "I knows a pirate craft when I sees one."

Pirates! Bethany felt a wave of faintness sweep over her, for this was a nightmare worse than all the rest. Yet nightmare it was. It must be. Such reality, with all that it implied, was too horrifying to contemplate.

There was a sudden stir of movement among the ruffians crowding close at Roach's back, and another man shouldered his way forward. He spun the last of his fellows roughly aside and stood staring at Bethany as though he could not believe what he saw. A tall young man, dark-haired, with light gray eyes in a lean, haughty face. The man whom, at such cost to herself, she had freed from slavery in Barbados two years before.

Now Bethany knew that she was dreaming, because the dream was so familiar and so dear. As Jared came to her, she waited for the awakening which always followed, bringing its sense of unutterable loneliness and loss, but this time she did not wake. The touch of his hands was warm on her shoulders, his voice was speaking her name in a tone which betrayed a disbelief as great as her own. With a sob she flung herself into his arms, her hands clutching at him, her body pressed close against his, for only by physical contact could she assure herself of reality. For the moment she did not question the how or the why of his presence aboard the *Santa Maria*; he was there, and that was enough.

Lucas Roach watched their meeting with an astonishment which was rapidly replaced by chagrin. Had Bethany known it, she had, by recoiling from him and then casting herself so joyfully into the arms of his comrade, committed two unpardonable offenses. She had wounded Roach's vanity, which was enormous; and she had made a mockery of his authority as captain, of which, having seized and held it by sheer brutality, he was inordinately jealous.

"Here's a meeting of old friends, it seems!" he remarked jeeringly, some of the fury he felt grating in his voice. "Or else the lady fancies she is free to make her own choice among us."

Jared looked at him above Bethany's disheveled golden head. "In Barbados she saved my life and gave me freedom," he said quietly, "and if you offer her even the smallest insult, Roach, I swear I will kill you."

Though he had not raised his voice, the words were heard clearly enough by those immediately about him, and several significant glances were exchanged. It was common knowledge among the buccaneer crew that little love was lost between Lucas Roach and Jared Vernon, but this was the first time that the younger man had openly challenged the captain. They waited expectantly to see what would follow.

"She may have been your doxy then," Roach said grimly, "but you are not in Barbados now, my friend! Among the Brethren, any woman taken belongs by right to all of us, like any other plunder."

"Any woman taken aboard a captured ship," Jared retorted, "but this lady, like her companions, is a castaway, victim of last night's storm."

"And if this man knew her in Barbados," Pendlecombe put in quickly, "he'll bear out what I says of her father's wealth. I reckon Mr. Court'll pay handsome to have her returned to him safe and sound."

Bethany listened fearfully to the argument. She had accepted at last the reality of Jared's presence, but if the dream were fact, so, too, was the nightmare. She was aboard a buccaneer ship, and she knew enough about these lawless sea-rovers to realize the danger in which she stood. Even if she had not known, she could have read it in the faces of the men about her, and especially in the evil, simian countenance of their captain; no consideration of pity or of chivalry would restrain him.

Jared was equally conscious of the peril. How Bethany came to be in her present plight he could not imagine, nor was it for the moment important. The only thing that mattered was to protect her from his cut-throat comrades. There had been women aboard the *Santa Maria* when they captured her—the captain's wife and daughter and a maidservant—and it was unimaginable that Bethany should suffer as those Spanish women had suffered until death set them free. Unaided, he could not prevent it by force; perhaps he could do so by guile.

"It is true that her father is a rich man," he agreed, addressing the staring, muttering crew. "You all know what wealth the sugar-planters of Barbados command, and Matthew Court owns one of the largest plantations in the colony. He'll pay, right enough, to have his daughter safely returned to him. Think on it, lads! There are wenches enough in the islands for your pleasure, and it is not often that a golden prize like this one drops into our hands."

There was a murmur of agreement, drowning the few dissentient voices. The buccaneers were always greedy for gold, and a ransom would be shared equally, so that all might profit, which, if their captain's will prevailed, they would not. In theory, what Roach said of the laws of the Brotherhood was true enough; in practice, as his followers knew from experience, the woman would become the property of the captain alone. Their inclination, therefore, was to side with Jared, and Roach knew it. He mastered his fury, and adopted a sarcastic tone.

"And who's to collect this ransom you prate of?

Are we to sail into Bridgetown harbor to demand it?
We'd not sail out again if we did!"

That gave them pause. Fifteen, twenty years ago,
when Henry Morgan and his men were pouring
Spanish loot to the value of hundreds of thousands of
pounds into Port Royal in Jamaica, they might have
risked it, but now the heyday of buccaneering was
over. Colonial governors no longer granted commis-
sions to buccaneer captains, and Morgan himself, as
Lieutenant-Governor of Jamaica, had engaged—
officially, at least—in putting down the "sweet trade
of piracy."

Roach, sensing the hesitation his words had
provoked, was quick to press his advantage. "They'd
not part with the ransom until we handed over the
wench, and once that was done, what's to prevent
them turning the guns of the fort on us as we put to
sea again? Dead men have no use for gold!"

It was an unanswerable argument. They had fared
exceptionally well during their present cruise, first
taking the *Santa Maria* with their own ship sinking
beneath them, and then, aided by the superior size
and armament of their prize, making several other
captures, approaching their unsuspecting prey under
Spanish colors and striking without warning. The
lure of yet more profit was tempting, but the difficulty
which Roach had pointed out undeniable.

He was grinning in anticipation of triumph, his
eyes gloating on the girl so that she shuddered and
turned her face against Jared's shoulder, while Jared
himself dropped a hand to the butt of the pistol he
carried. Roach's glance followed the movement, and
the grin widened a fraction as he laid his hands on
his own weapon. He knew that Vernon would not risk
an exchange of shots with the woman in his arms,
and so he counted victory already won. Jared's next
words took him completely by surprise.

"What Roach says is true," he admitted, raising

his voice so that all might hear, "but the profit can be yours without the risk. I will stand proxy for Matthew Court, and ransom his daughter from you here and now."

There was a moment of astonished silence, and then the quartermaster, always the acknowledged spokesman of the men, asked warily: "What d'ye offer for her?"

"My whole share of the profits of this cruise," Jared replied promptly. "The gold and jewels which have already been divided you may have now, and I will claim no part in the price obtained for the rest of the cargo when it is sold in Tortuga. In return, she will remain under my protection alone until I can restore her to her family."

There was some derisive laughter at that, indicating that they believed he had no such intention, and the quartermaster said bluntly:

"That's a price *I'd* not pay for any wench, no matter how comely, but if you've that much of a mind to her, Vernon, take her and welcome. What say you, lads?"

There was a chorus of agreement; Roach tried to protest, but was shouted down, for in that respect, at least, the buccaneers bowed to no authority. They tolerated Lucas Roach as their captain because he led them to rich profit, but, except when in action, they made their own decisions, and Roach was a man who inspired neither loyalty nor liking. Jared, on the other hand, was popular among them, and if he was prepared to pay generously for the privilege of keeping the girl for himself, they were willing to accept the bargain.

Roach himself was shrewd enough not to press the matter. He shrugged and turned away, assuming an indifference he did not feel, but not before Jared had read a warning of future treachery in his eyes. He would need, he knew, to be constantly on his guard where Lucas Roach was concerned, but at least a respite had been gained, and Bethany's immediate danger was over.

"Come," he said gently, and led her away aft, paying no heed to the good-natured ribaldries of his fellow buccaneers.

She went with him unquestioningly, along the gangway and into the great cabin, where he threw open the door of one of the smaller cabins which led out of it.

"These are my own quarters," he said. "You will be safe here."

For the first time she seemed to realize that they were alone, for she lifted her drooping head and looked dazedly about her. Her face was ashen with weariness and strain; her hair, still wet with sea-water, clung to her forehead and tumbled down her back over the drenched ruin of her beautiful gown; her voice, when at length she spoke, was husky and exhausted.

"Jared, I do not understand! How you come to be here, what is going to happen...!"

"There will be time enough later to talk of that," he broke in gently, taking her hands and folding them between his own. "I give you my word that you are in no danger. There is a bolt inside the cabin door, and I promise that I shall not be far away, so go now and rest."

Bethany knew that he was right. She had reached the end of her endurance, for the cabin seemed to be spinning crazily around her and Jared's voice sounded as though he were speaking a long way away. It required an enormous effort even to go past him into the smaller cabin, to turn, as he drew the door shut behind her, and shoot the bolt into place.

In the great cabin, Jared stood for some time deep in thought. Bethany was too exhausted now to care much about what had happened, and it would have

been brutal to try to question her, but when the
physical effects of her ordeal had passed she would
have to face the truth. She must have been traveling
with her husband, but Warren would never voluntari-
ly have parted from her, and since there was no sign
of any other survivors of the shipwreck, he must have
been drowned when the ship went down. Bereavement would be yet another burden added to that
which she already had to bear.

He walked across to the table in the middle of the
cabin and flung himself into the chair at the head of
it, wondering how he was to achieve his avowed
purpose and restore Bethany safely to Barbados.
Then suddenly an odd circumstance struck him and
he sat upright, the frown deepening between his
brows. Bethany's hands, resting passively in his,
had been entirely bare of adornment. She wore no
wedding ring.

Jared said: "Do not imagine that you are in any
sense a prisoner, but I would prefer you to remain
behind the locked door of your cabin unless I can be
with you."

"I would prefer it, too," Bethany replied in a low
voice, "but I do not wish to deprive you of your
quarters."

"That is of no importance. What *is* important is
that you should keep out of Roach's way. The other
men, I think, will abide by the bargain they made
with me, for the Brethren of the Coast usually honor
agreements with their own kind, but Lucas Roach
has not even a rogue's honor."

It was the following day and they were in the great
cabin, Bethany seated on the stern-locker while
Jared stood beside her. Though she was still pale, her
eyes shadowed by memory of the ordeal through
which she had lately passed, rest and food had done

much to restore her; now, lacking the blind acceptance of the situation which exhaustion had induced,
she was conscious of awkwardness. Recollection of
their parting two years before, and the reunion the
previous day, made her feel suddenly shy, and she
shrank from disclosing to him all that happened
since their last meeting. To postpone a little longer
the need to do so, she asked anxiously:

"Jared, what is going to happen? What will
become of me?"

"I trust that eventually you will be safely restored
to your home, but at present I am not certain how that
may be accomplished. Meanwhile, I must ask you to
accept my protection—and I thank God that I am
here to offer it."

"Do you suppose *I* do not give thanks for it also?"
she asked reproachfully. "But, Jared, how *do* you
come to be here? I have imagined you back in Holland
these many months."

He shrugged. "That was my intention, but before I
could continue the journey which, with your aid, I
had begun, it was necessary to obtain the means to do
so. In Curaçao I found it easy enough to find
employment for my sword, but before I had accumulated enough money to buy a passage to Europe, I
began to ask myself why I was troubling to do so.
England is closed to me. Holland, although my
mother's native land, is no more my home than any
other country. Here in the Indies is work enough for a
professional soldier, so here I resolved to stay."

"But you are not in Dutch service now," she
protested. "This is a buccaneer ship."

"I had already seen service with the Dutch navy,"
he explained, "and so I chose to serve again at the
sea. You must know how fine a line is drawn in these
waters between lawful privateering, and piracy. It is
all too easy to drift from one to the other. Besides"—
he laughed with wry self-mockery—"it seems that in

spite of everything, I am still more English than Dutch. I craved the company of my own countrymen, but, being outlawed, can associate only with those of them who are also beyond the Law."

He paused, but when she did not reply, or look at him, the amusement faded from his face. He reached out and tilted her head up towards him, forcing her to meet his eyes.

"Disillusioned, Bethany? Do you think the worse of me for debasing my sword to the plunder of Spanish ships and Spanish settlements? A far cry, is it not, from championing the cause of Protestant England against Royal tyranny?"

"I hope," she retorted with a flash of spirit, "that I am not fool enough to condemn any man for so slight a cause. I was born in the Indies, remember, and know how great a debt is owed to the buccaneers. But, Jared, this Captain Roach! Do you indeed crave the comradeship of such as he? A man, as you have just said, lacking even a rogue's honor."

"No," he agreed ruefully, "my judgment was at fault there. Roach has a high reputation among the buccaneers, and indeed is one of the most successful, but had I known the full vileness of the fellow, I would never have sailed with him. Acquit me on that score, at least."

She smiled fleetingly. "I have no right to reproach you, nor any cause that I know of. Even if I had, how could I do so, when I am so greatly in your debt?"

"Did we not agree long ago that there should be no talk between us of debts and repayment?" She did not reply and after a moment he continued in a graver tone: "I have answered all your questions, Bethany, and asked none of you. Must I do so?"

"No. I will tell you." She spoke in a low voice, her whole attention apparently centered on the hopeless task of trying to smooth some of the creases from the stained and faded silk of her skirt. "I am not married.

Pierce…" Her voice faltered and then steadied again. "Pierce refused to take me for his wife after Will Hopson told what he had seen."

"Warren believed him?" Jared's disbelief was so great that it left no room, as yet, for anger. "He took the word of a servant, whom he knew to hold a grudge against you, rather than yours?"

"Not the servants' word alone. Hopson merely spread the story. Someone else convinced Pierce—and my father—that it was true."

"Miss Esther!" Jared's tone made the words a statement rather than a question, and sheer astonishment caused Bethany to look up at him.

"How did you guess that?"

"Who else could claim certain knowledge of such a matter? Who else would have been believed? And your sister was jealous of you."

She shook her head wonderingly. "I do not understand how you could know that. I did not even suspect it myself."

"How could she fail to be jealous, when you excel her in every way? I would not have thought, though, that she had malice enough, or courage enough, to attack you."

Bethany sighed. "The chance offered, and she took it. She told me that herself." She hesitated for a moment. "Pierce married her soon afterwards. They have a baby son."

Jared said, under his breath, something extremely uncomplimentary both to Pierce Warren and to his wife, and then added, more audibly, an abrupt question. "Why did you leave Barbados?"

There was a pause. Bethany's trembling fingers were still pulling at the silk, pulling so hard that the fine stuff, rotted by sun and sea-water, tore slighty beneath the strain. She moved her hands in a little, exasperated gesture and then clasped them tightly together.

"We have kinfolk in Jamaica. My father thought it best that I should go to live with them for a time."

"Best for whom?" Jared asked dryly.

Bethany hesitated. Not even to him could she reveal how deeply she had suffered, or speak of the humiliations which, even now, made her cringe with remembered shame. The women, from Governor's lady to bondservant, raking her with sharp, appraising glances, wondering if she were with child and visibly disappointed when they realized that their suspicions were unfounded. The endless slights, the grudging civility in place of friendly welcome, the certainty that even this much was granted her only for the sake of her father and sister. The men, their former deference entirely gone, treating her with a familiarity they would never have dared to use before, and then, when she repulsed their advances with outraged indignation, implying—or even actually saying—that since she had made free with a slave she was placing an undue value on her favors now.

"For all of us," she said reluctantly at length. "Oh, believe me, Jared, I was not sorry to go!"

He realized that she meant it, and the mere fact that she had been glad to leave her home enabled him to guess something of what she had endured on his account. Unaccustomed remorse shook him, for though he could not have protected her even by sacrificing his chance of escape, as Bethany herself had so clearly seen at the time, he had taken all and given nothing in return. Only now, with the abrupt reversal of their fortunes, could he do anything to make amends, and even that could not erase the past.

"It seems unbelievable that your father accepted these lies," he said slowly. "I would have been ready to swear he would stand by you, no matter who else might doubt. Did you not tell him that your sister was lying?"

"I was given no chance. Both he and Pierce accepted her word without question, before I had a chance to speak in my own defense. Any protest I might have made would only have seemed like further evidence of my guilt, and besides, if they were so ready to believe that I had sinned, I could not humble myself and beg them to believe me innocent."

He nodded, for this was something he could understand. She was both proud and sensitive, and when that sensitivity was wounded, pride would make it imperative that she hide the wound. She would endure rather than plead for mercy. In that, at least, he and she were alike.

Looking at her, he could see how suffering had set its mark upon her. She was truly beautiful now, with a depth and maturity which the unclouded happiness of girlhood had lacked, and which shone even through her present disarray. It was no wonder that Roach's evil passion had been aroused by the mere sight of her. Nor had her danger ended with Jared's own bargain with the crew; it would continue as long as she was within the captain's reach, for no man could be ceaselessly vigilant, and there were so many ways in which death could come by stealth. He had learned long ago, as a soldier must, to look death in the face, but now the fear of dying clawed at him as it had not done for years, for his death would leave Bethany wholly unprotected. And he loved her, had loved her even before he left Barbados. That was why freedom had seemed an empty prize, and why he had lingered in the Indies, reluctant to put half the width of the world between them even though he believed they would never meet again.

Until that moment he had not known, or, at least, had refused to acknowledge, what it was that ailed him, but now the knowledge forced itself upon him against his will. He who for most of his adult life had avoided any close human relationship was caught in the trap of emotions he had always distrusted, but, even as he recognized the fact, he recognized also that it did not alter the situation in the slightest degree. All that mattered was to keep her safe, and to restore her eventually to her family. No matter how long that took, however difficult it proved to be, his own feelings must be subordinated to that one aim. By allowing her to endure so much on his behalf he had already been guilty of a kind of betrayal; he must not be so again.

It would not be easy. Since they were to be constantly in each other's company, and she completely dependent upon him, for an indefinite period of time, his attitude towards her must remain as it had been when he was her servant in Barbados; their parting, their reunion the previous day, must be put out of mind, ignored as though it had never happened. Only thus could he hope to abide by his resolve.

He turned abruptly away and picked up from the table a pair of pistols supported one at either end of a strip of leather shaped like a priest's stole. Taking one of the weapons from its holster, he said in a matter-of-fact tone:

"There will be times when I cannot be at hand to protect you, so you must have the means to defend yourself should danger threaten. I will give you a pistol, and you must keep it by you always, as long as we are aboard this ship."

Bethany eyed the weapon distrustfully. "I do not know how to use it."

"I am going to teach you. This one is unloaded, and can do no harm. Come, take it."

Reluctantly she obeyed. Jared sat beside her on the locker and showed her how the gun was fired, patiently repeating the lesson until he was sure she had grasped the rudiments of it. Then he drew the other pistol and handed it to her.

"This one is loaded and primed. Keep it always near you, and do not hesitate to use it should the need arise."

She took it gingerly. "I do not suppose I would hit anything I aimed at, even if I tried."

"At close quarters you would not find it difficult," he replied grimly, and took her free hand in his own. "Bethany, it is Roach I am thinking of. If he molests you, use that pistol on him with no more compunction than you would feel at using it on a wild animal. He deserves no better."

She shivered, remembering the shambling, ape-like figure of the buccaneer captain. Yet could she bring herself to shoot another human being, even such a one as Lucas Roach, and even in her own defense? She did not know, and could only pray that she would never have to make the decision.

Lucas Roach was in an evil humor, and most of its venom was directed against Jared Vernon. They had been at odds almost from the first, for Vernon, to Roach's way of thinking, had far too many scruples for a true buccaneer, even though he fought well and his military experience by land and sea was a valuable asset.

There had been, for example, the absurd business of the three Spanish women. He had tried to protect them, even suggesting that they should be restored to their home, which had almost precipitated a riot among the crew. They would probably have hacked him to pieces had not the quartermaster, Rob Haddon, knocked him on the head and confined him below decks until their fury abated. In the light of later events, Captain Roach felt that Haddon had been needlessly merciful.

Haddon, however, was no more an admirer of the captain than Vernon was, and an alliance between them was the last thing Roach desired. He knew that his position was precarious. He might talk, when it suited him, of the traditional equality of the buccaneers, but he had gradually usurped more and more authority, despising the superstitious, uneducated seamen who were his comrades, and certain of his own superiority over them. Lucas Roach had been born a gentleman, and not all the crime and villainy in which he had wallowed for years had quite eradicated his inherent arrogance. That, perhaps, was the origin of his hatred of Jared.

It was a hatred which might never have come to a head but for the advent of Bethany Court. Roach had not even glimpsed the girl during the three days she had been aboard his ship, but the recollection of her was a constant torment, and he was determined to possess her. The only consideration which had so far restrained him was how to accomplish his purpose with no risk to himself.

It was not only Vernon he had to take into account. He would have had no hesitation in killing Jared had the younger man been the only obstacle in his way, but there was also Rob Haddon and, behind him, the rest of the crew, who had entered into an agreement with Vernon. Where Haddon was concerned Roach knew that he must tread warily. Aboard a buccaneer ship the quartermaster had an authority he enjoyed nowhere else. In importance he was second only to the captain; it was he who shared out the plunder, and to whom all disputes were referred; he was usually, as in Haddon's case, a veteran seaman skilled in navigation. Such a man was the crew's champion against a captain's tyranny, and Roach knew that the patience of his men had already been tried to the uttermost.

Yet have the girl he must. The thought of her haunted him, giving him no peace, and Lucas Roach was not accustomed to subduing his desires. Yet how to achieve his purpose? She had never ventured on deck; unless Vernon was with her she remained shut in her cabin, and he knew, for he had tried the door, that it was always barred. For days he had brooded over the problem, but now, pacing moodily to and fro across the poop deck, he began to perceive a solution.

That night, when he knew that Jared was on watch, he made his way furtively to the great cabin. Very softly he tried Bethany's door, and, as he had expected, found that it was barred from within. He shrugged, and, crossing to the open stern-ports, clambered out on to the narrow gallery below the counter. Far below him, faintly phosphorescent in the moonlight, slid the foaming water of the ship's wake, but Roach had nerves of iron and the agility of the ape he so closely resembled, and his precarious perch held no terrors for him. He edged his way along the gallery until he reached the port belonging to the girl's cabin, which was open but curtained within, for the *Santa Maria*, like so many Spanish ships, was luxuriously appointed. Very cautiously, clinging to his perch with one hand, he reached through and parted the curtains just enough to afford him a glimpse of the interior, which was illuminated by a lamp swinging from the rafters.

Bethany was preparing to retire for the night. She had laid aside the torn and faded gown of amber silk with its stiff, tight-laced bodice, and the sea-stained petticoat embroidered with green and gold; now she knelt, absorbed in prayer, before the crucifix fastened to the bulkhead above the bed. It was a Popish emblem from which, at another time, she would have turned in dismay, but aboard this godless ship it gave at once reassurance and hope. In her desperate plight, it even seemed symbolic that the holy emblem had been left untouched when the buccaneers ransacked their prize, though the reason for its immunity was prosaic enough. The crucifix was exquisitely carved, a miniature work of art, but it was made of wood, with no ornamentation of gold or precious stones, and therefore, in the eyes of the buccaneers, completely valueless.

Engrossed in her devotions, Bethany was unaware of the man peering at her between the curtains of the port. For a full minute he crouched there, exulting over what he saw, his little, evil eyes feasting upon her. On the unbound hair, bright as gold in the lamplight; the white shoulders rising from the creamy silk shift with its bedraggled lace; the graceful, rounded body half glimpsed beneath the clinging silk. Then he flung the curtains apart and with one agile, twisting movement was through the port and into the cabin.

The girl's head jerked up, her blue eyes wide with astonishment and alarm, her lips parted for a scream she seemed unable to utter, and thus for the space of a heartbeat they confronted each other, she still upon her knees, he poised like a crouching beast below the port. Then she flung herself forward, snatched the pistol from under the pillow and fired in blind panic.

Roach's reaction at sight of the weapon was quicker than conscious thought, an instinctive response born of years of danger faced and survived. He dropped to his knees, and the ball passed harmlessly over his head to bury itself in the bulkhead close to the port.

Through the drifting smoke of the shot Bethany saw him rising to his feet, and in terror flung the empty pistol at him with all her strength and sprang to the door. Her trembling fingers found and drew the bolt, and then he was upon her.

She did scream then, with terror and with loathing, fighting to free herself from the great arms, clawing and striking with futile desperation at his face and chest. Roach cursed, but his hold did not slacken. He knew that he had blundered. He had

known it from the instant the shot rang out; the pistol
had taken him completely by surprise, for it had
never even crossed his mind that she might be armed,
and he was aware that the sound must have given the
alarm. That thought had been in his mind as he leapt
to prevent her escape, but now that he held her, every
consideration of caution, and even the instinct of
self-preservation, was swept aside, and all that
mattered was to overcome her resistance.

So blind and deaf was he to all else that even the
clatter of approaching footsteps failed to distract
him, and when the door crashed open to admit Jared,
with several other men at his heels, it did not even
occur to him to make Bethany a hostage for his own
escape. With a snarl of rage he scrambled up and
braced himself to meet the younger man's attack.

Roach wore no sword, nor would there have been
room for swordplay in the tiny cabin. Jared, fully
aware of the adversary with whom he had to deal,
came at him with a knife, but the captain met him
emptyhanded, confident in his own enormous
strength. He foiled the first blow by grabbing Jared's
upraised arm about the wrist; the knife clattered to
the deck, but Jared twisted free and dealt Roach two
terrific blows which would have felled an ordinary
man. Roach merely grunted and lunged at him again,
while the men in the doorway shouted advice and
encouragement, and Bethany, now kneeling upright
on the bed with her torn shift clutched about her,
watched with horrified eyes, appalled by the bestial
savagery of the fight.

Jared had had no opportunity to recover his knife,
and he knew that, unarmed, he had no hope of
prevailing. He was strong and active, but Roach was
abnormally powerful and more than capable of
killing with his bare hands; it was his boast that he
had never yet found a man who could overpower him.
There remained to Jared only his sword, and, with

Bethany's safety at stake he could no longer be governed by any sentimental consideration of honor. He sprang back and attempted to draw the weapon, but before it was half out of his scabbard Roach had grappled with him.

As the crushing grip of those tremendous arms closed about him Jared knew that he had failed. He continued to fight with every ounce of his strength, but the taste of defeat was bitter in his mouth, and the thought of Bethany an agony in his mind. His resistance threw Roach off balance and they crashed together to the deck, but the terrible grip never slackened. Slowly, remorselessly, it was crushing out his life; he could scarcely draw breath; the blood was drumming in his ears, and the ugly, evil face above him began to waver as though seen through water.

The men in the doorway fell silent. Their sympathies might be with Jared, but this was a fight to the death for possession of a woman, and the strange code of their fierce brotherhood forbade them to intervene. Bethany, still crouched in the bed, had forgotten her own danger and could think only of Jared's. Had the loaded pistol still been to hand she would have used it on Roach without hesitation or pity, but as it was she could only watch with anguished eyes.

Jared's hand moved blindly, gropingly across the deck, vainly seeking some hold, some leverage which might enable him to break free. Instead it encountered something smooth and sharp, and slowly into his clouded mind came the realization that this was the blade of his knife. He fumbled for the handle, felt his fingers close clumsily about it, and with the last of his failing strength lifted the weapon and drove it to the hilt between Roach's ribs.

The buccaneer uttered a choking gasp, and his murderous grip relaxed as he half rose, clutching instinctively at the wound. For a second or two he pawed blindly at the hilt of the knife protruding bloodily from his side, and then a sudden spasm stiffened his body and he pitched forward, pinning Jared beneath him.

So sudden and unexpected had been the reversal of the situation that at first the watching men could only gape foolishly. Then one of them—it was John Pendlecombe—stepped forward and began to drag the captain's body aside. Another man moved to help him, and Jared, relieved of the crushing weight, was able to struggle to his knees, and then, clinging to the bed for support, to his feet. He could scarcely stand, and his chest heaved as he fought for every rasping breath, but he laid his hands on his sword and placed himself before Bethany to shield her from the men's gaze, and from any move which might be made towards her.

Rob Haddon thrust his way through the knot of men in the doorway. For a few tense moments he and Jared faced each other in a silence taut as a bowstring, and then the quartermaster's glance shifted to the uncouth corpse at his feet. He considered it dispassionately, and shrugged.

"Heave that carrion over the side," he said callously. "He's come by his just deserts for breaking the agreement."

Promptly, almost with relief, they hastened to obey him, for until a new captain was chosen the quartermaster's word would be law. Haddon stepped aside while they dragged the body away and then he looked again at Jared, a steady exchange of glances which seemed, without any need for words, to establish an understanding between them. Then he turned and went out, pulling the door shut behind him.

Jared wiped his forearm across his streaming brow. The agony of drawing breath was lessening, but his mind still felt leaden, his thoughts moving sluggishly. Haddon's intervention had given the men a lead, averting for the time being any further move against Jared or the girl, but the situation was still potentially dangerous. It was imperative he should know what they were saying, what was being decided among them. Wearily he straightened his shoulders and was moving towards the door when, behind him, Bethany spoke in a shaken whisper.

"Jared, do not leave me! Do not leave me alone!"

"I must!" Slowly he turned back to the bed where she still knelt, white-faced and trembling. "I must be sure that Haddon's will prevails, and that they still honor the bargain struck when they let me ransom you. There may be others among them of Roach's mind, now that he is dead."

"And now that they have seen you again," he added in his thoughts. "Now that they have had this glimpse of you to spur their lust." She was looking piteously up at him, her face death-pale below the crown of bright, disordered hair, and he was shaken again by fury at what Roach had intended, what he had dared to attempt.

With a stifled exclamation he caught her in his arms, and she yielded utterly to his embrace, her arms going about him, her warm lips answering his kisses. With that wordless surrender she gave herself trustfully, completely into his keeping, and to turn from her was the hardest thing he had ever done; but the world was not bounded by the confines of this small, dimly lighted cabin, nor inhabited by them alone. He drew back and looked down again into her face.

"Bar the door after me," he said huskily. "I will have John Pendlecombe stand guard in the great

cabin till morning, for him, at least, we can trust. Try
not to be afraid, my love! God did not bring us
together again without purpose, and, with His aid, I
will yet take you safely home."

He freed himself gently from her clinging arms
and went quickly out of the cabin, knowing beyond
doubt that if he lingered, even for a moment, he would
be unable to resist the temptation to stay. Bethany,
forgetting to bar the door as he had bidden her, sank
back upon the pillow and lay gazing up at the carved
and painted rafters, the horror of Roach's attack
upon her, and his violent death, fading now before a
deep, all-pervading happiness. Jared did love her.
His aloofness during the past few days had puzzled
and saddened her, but now all pretence between them
was over.

In the light of the truth now revealed, even her own
disgrace during the past two years wore a different
aspect. She would never quite forget the humiliations
she had suffered, just as Jared would never completely forget the shame of his slavery, yet had she
not had to suffer it, she would never have been
reunited with him. He was right to see God's hand in
that, and his victory over Lucas Roach was yet
another instance of Divine mercy. "I will take you
safely home," he had said, but her home now was
where he chanced to be, and she would go with him
gladly wherever he wished. It was all she asked of
life—that they should not be parted again.

At last she slept, and when she opened her eyes
again there was sunlight streaming between the
curtains. As memory of the night returned, she sat
upright, listening apprehensively, but everything
was quiet. Ominously quiet, perhaps? She slipped
from the bed and stole across to set her ear to the
crack of the door, but only the creak of timbers and
the slap of water against the ship's side distrubed the

silence. Her glance fell on the drawn bolt, and she slid it guiltily into place.

Hurriedly she dressed, wondering whether she dare venture out to try to discover what had happened after the death of Lucas Roach, and to allay her fears on Jared's behalf. Before she was ready to leave the cabin, however, a knock on the door made her jump, and then Jared's voice called her name.

Trembling with relief, she replied breathlessly, and, abandoning the hopeless task of trying to bind up her hair, threw open the door. Without shyness or hesitation she went straight into his arms, neither knowing nor caring whether or not he were alone, and only after that first glad embrace did she look about her. Save for themselves, the great cabin was empty. She looked anxiously at him.

"Is all well? Are you?"

He laughed, shrugging the latter question aside. He was stiff and sore from his mauling by Lucas Roach, and to draw a deep breath still caused him acute discomfort, but he had no intention of letting Bethany know it. So he answered the first part of her question instead.

"With Roach dead, the worst of the danger is past. The men have elected Rob Haddon as captain, and he has given me his word that the bargain I made with them will be honored. Have no fear he cannot keep his promise. Roach was hated, and remained captain only because no one dared challenge him. Haddon the men respect."

He could have added, had he wished, that since his own victory over Lucas Roach, the men respected him also, for more than one of their comrades had died at Roach's hands in quarrels of various kinds. Jared himself knew how much he owed his triumph to the chance recovery of his knife, but the more the buccaneers respected his prowess, the safer Bethany would be, and he intended to take full advantage of the fact.

She was only partly reassured by his reply. "But what is going to happen now?"

"We are going to take breakfast together," he replied lightly, and led her to the table, where food and drink from the *Santa Maria*'s ample stores was set. "Haddon practices that true buccaneering equality which Roach merely preached, and shares meals and quarters with the men, so we need fear no intrusion."

It was clear that he intended to answer no further questions at present, and Bethany was willing enough to abandon them also, and to give herself up to the happiness of the moment. To snatch, from the difficulties and dangers which still beset them, one precious hour when the friendship which had grown between them in Barbados, and the love which had flowered from it, merged into a companionship perfect and undemanding. When it was sufficient simply to be together; to talk or to be silent; to glance up and smile into one another's eyes, or to let hands meet briefly across the table. A time which could not have come to them before, and would never, in quite the same way, come again. A time made doubly precious by its very transience.

When the meal was over they sat on the locker by the open stern-ports, Bethany with Jared's arms about her, her head resting against his shoulder. She was utterly happy, utterly content, as, idly, she asked the question which was to shatter contentment for ever.

"Jared, whither are we bound?"

There was a pause, a long pause, before he replied, and then he said very quietly: "For Barbados."

"Barbados?" Bethany could not believe that she had heard him correctly. She sat upright, swinging round to face him. "You cannot be serious!"

"Completely! Did I not tell you that, with God's aid, I would take you safely home?"

"But you cannot!" Her eyes, dark with dismay, were desperately searching his face for some hint that he spoke in jest. Searching in vain. "You cannot," she faltered again.

"I must," he replied in a low voice. "I have no choice."

"I understand!" She sprang up and went to stand by the table with her back to him, gripping the back of a chair hard with both hands. "I have taken too much for granted! I thought...!"

"You thought I loved you," Jared broke in, "and now you think I do not." He got up also and came to her, turning her to face him again. "Bethany, do you not see that is why I *must* take you home? Because, for the first time in my life, I have learned to love someone better than myself?"

"But *you* cannot return to Barbados," she whispered. "If I go back, I must go alone. Oh, Jared, do not ask that of me!"

"What else can I ask?" he said bitterly. "That you marry me? I have no money, no home—no country, even! Where would we live? Among the buccaneers of Tortuga, the logwood-cutters of Campeachy? Do you think I would drag you down to that?"

"We could go to Curacao, or some other Dutch colony. Your buccaneering would not be held against you."

"No, but that would mean living in poverty, for a man of my present calling amasses no wealth. What he wins at sea he spends as soon as he goes ashore, and...!"

"And all your plunder from this present cruise you pledged to buy my safety," she broke in softly. "Jared, I am not afraid of being poor."

He gave a faint, rueful smile, and lifted his hand to her tumbled hair, pushing it back from her face. "You do not even know what it means," he said tenderly. "You who have been lapped in luxury since the day you were born. And this would be poverty in exile, my love. In a strange land, cut off completely from your family, with no one to turn to in time of trouble, or to look after you if I should die. You have no knowledge of what such isolation can mean, even when there is no poverty to add to the burden, but I have. My mother spent half her life thus."

"Perhaps she counted it worth the cost," Bethany protested. "She must have loved your father, to go into exile for his sake."

"My father!" Jared's voice was suddenly harsh, and to her dismay, she saw his expression harden until he looked as he looked the first time she saw him, angry and contemptuous. "Yes, God pity her! She loved him!"

He let her go and swung away to stare from the stern-ports, while Bethany, a little frightened by that abrupt change of mood, watched him in distress. At length she said tentatively:

"Jared, what is it? What have I said?" She moved closer to him and laid a timid hand on his arm. "I did not mean to hurt or anger you."

"Of course you did not." He covered her hand with his own and looked down at her, forcing a smile. "What you said was innocent enough." He hesitated, frowning a little, and then went on abruptly: "Bethany, do you remember I once told you my reason for offering my sword to Monmouth?"

She nodded. "You said that, had he triumphed, you might have achieved a purpose otherwise impossible to fulfil; but you never told me what that purpose was."

"I will tell you now." His voice was still harsh with bitterness, the gray eyes somber. "The chance I sought, the purpose which took me back to England, was to bring about my father's utter ruin and destruction."

She stared at him in horror. "Jared! In God's name, why?"

"Because I hate him more than any living being who walks this earth!" Jared spoke with suppressed passion, and then, seeing her expression, laughed shortly, without amusement. "You cannot believe that, can you? Even now, when your own father has condemned you unheard, you cannot begin to comprehend what it is like so to hate the man who begot you."

"No, I do not hate my father," she said quietly. "I love him. That is why it hurts me unbearably that he has turned against me."

"Any why you find it almost impossible to believe what I have just told you?" he added as she paused. "Wait, then, until you have heard the whole story, and can judge for yourself."

Her hand still rested in his. He led her back to the stern-locker and made her sit down, but remained standing himself, looking out at the empty, glittering sea. In the brilliant, reflected light the grimness of his lean, dark face was very apparent.

"My father is the Earl of St. Orme," he said after a moment. "During the years following the execution of the King he was active in Royalist conspiracies, and eventually was obliged to seek refuge abroad.

His travels took him, in the course of time, to Holland,
and there in the first months of 1660, he met my
mother.

"She was just fifteen and at that time, I believe,
very beautiful. Beautiful enough, in any event, to
inflame St. Orme's desire, and he began a determined
pursuit of her. Her father, a prosperous merchant,
mistrusted him and forbade her to see him, but by
this time she was in love with the Earl, even though
he was twenty years older than she. Being young and
innocent, she believed him when he swore he loved
her also, and when it became possible, with the
restoration of King Charles, for him to return home,
he had no difficulty in persuading her to go with him,
promising her marriage once England was reached.

"He established her in a lodging in London, in the
care of a servant who had been with him in Holland,
and since she spoke scarcely any English, it was
some time before she discovered the truth. St. Orme
had been married for years; he had children as old as
she, and his wife was still living."

Bethany uttered a little sound of pity and distress,
her ready compassion stirred by the thought of that
unfortunate girl so callously betrayed. "You mean he
abandoned her?"

"By no means. He made what he considered to be
generous provision for her. He had promised her
marriage in England, and he kept his word. He
married her to his kinsman, Thomas Vernon."

Jared paused, but Bethany could find nothing to
say. This was the story which, for nearly three years,
she had been waiting and hoping to hear, but now,
watching his face as he told it, she wished for his sake
that the memories it evoked had been left undis-
turbed.

"You may consider," he resumed after a moment,
"that she ought to have refused, but remember, she
was only fifteen, alone and penniless in a foreign

land, knowing that she could never return to her family. She was also carrying St. Orme's child."

"And Thomas Vernon knew that?" Bethany's voice was incredulous.

"I do not wonder you find it hard to believe, but by the standards of King Charles's Court there was little unusual in such a bargain. Vernon was a man growing old, as broken in pride by the wars as in health and fortune. In return for becoming St. Orme's pensioner, he agreed to marry the Earl's mistress and give her bastard a name."

The words were spoken in a quiet, matter-of-fact tone, but an indescribable bitterness rang through them. Bethany, her heart torn by love and pity, stretched out her hand to touch his; for an instant there was no response, then his fingers closed about hers and he moved to sit beside her.

"It was inevitable, I suppose, that my stepfather should dislike me. St. Orme had settled upon him the manor of Abbotsmere in Kent, and my mother governed the household and looked well to his comfort, but I was a constant reminder of the source of that bounty." He was silent for a moment, looking down at their clasped hands. "As a child his indifference grieved me, for I believed myself truly his son, but as I grew older I began to suspect something of the truth. Remarks overheard by chance, knowing looks, sly jests only half understood—all these told me that our family was in some way different from those of our neighbors.

"Abbotsmere lay only a few miles from St. Orme's principal seat, and sometimes he passed through our village. Once, when I was twelve years old, I was watching him ride by when he drew rein and called me to him. He asked my name, and when I told him, he laughed, as though he had already guessed it, and tossed me a golden guinea. When I told my mother, I could not understand why she wept.

"When I was fifteen she became ill, and before long we realized that her illness was mortal. She herself knew it, and one day she told me the story I have just related to you. Then she asked me to go to St. Orme and beg him to visit her before she died. She had always loved him, you see, in spite of his betrayal of her."

"You went?" Bethany's voice was scarcely louder than a whisper.

"Yes. I went. My mother contrived to write to him, though she was so weak she could scarcely hold the pen, and I rode with the letter to St. Orme's great house. There I was passed from one disdainful lackey to another, and finally left to cool my heels while the letter was carried to the Earl. It was on that day I learned the reason for the hints and jests which had plagued my boyhood, for in the room where I waited was a portrait of St. Orme as a lad, and looking at it was like looking at my own face in a mirror. No wonder my stepfather resented me!"

"Did he not resent even more the Earl coming to visit your mother?"

"He might have done," Jared replied dryly, "if St. Orme had come."

Bethany gasped. "*If* he had...? You mean he refused?"

"He refused!" Jared's tone was bitter. "He did not even condescend to see me. After I had waited an unconscionable time there came yet another lackey— a chamberlain, or major-domo or something such— who told me that though his lordship was grieved to hear of Mrs. Vernon's illness, he was on the point of setting out for London, where his attendance at Court was required, and regretted therefore that he could not call upon her. My mother died two days later."

Bethany sought in vain for words to express what she felt. She could only tighten her clasp upon his hand with silent sympathy.

"After her death," he went on, "I could no longer endure life at Abbotsmere. It had long been my ambition to become a soldier, and, my stepfather being as glad to be rid of me as I was to go, a cornetcy in the army was obtained for me and I embarked upon a career which, I was convinced, would lead to greatness." He looked up, his face filled with grim self-mockery. "Whither it led me in fact you already know. Fugitive slave and outlawed pirate! That is the sum of my achievement!"

"There is no shame in misfortune, Jared," Bethany said gently. "Nor is worldly gain the sole measure of a man."

"Oh, do not think I rail against God or fate," he replied wearily. "Most of my misfortunes I have brought upon myself. But I can never forgive St. Orme for his betrayal of my mother, or his callousness when she lay dying, and I resolved then that I would make my own way in the world, with no further help from him. When my stepfather died four years later I went to St. Orme, forced my way into his presence, and flung the deeds of Abbotsmere in his face. It was a satisfaction I had dreamed of for years, but I would have done well to deny myself the pleasure it gave me. He broke me for it."

"How?" Bethany whispered, and Jared shrugged.

"He is a crony of King James—then the Duke of York—and it is easy enough for a man with influence in high places to discredit a junior officer. I was lucky to escape with my life.

"The rest is soon told. I fled from England and, since I spoke Dutch as fluently as my own tongue, took service in Holland until King Charles died and Monmouth resolved to challenge James's right to the throne. If James fell, St. Orme would fall with him, and that was enough to persuade me to take part in the rebellion. But James still rules, my father still enjoys his favor, and is like to do so for ever for all that I can do to prevent it." He hesitated, and then, when she did not immediately reply, added abruptly: "So now you have it! The whole truth! You may make your judgment."

Bethany looked at him, and saw, deep in his eyes, the anxiety his voice had not betrayed. Her own eyes were very bright, for tears were not far away. She could guess something of what it had cost a man so proud and self-sufficient to disclose so much, even to her whom he loved, and she was inexpressibly touched. She lifted her hand and gently touched his cheek.

"I am glad that you told me, Jared, for I understand now so much which puzzled me, but do not speak of judgment between us. I love you. That is all I know, all I care about." She leaned against him, pressing her face against his shoulder. "Let me stay with you! Do not send me away!"

"Do you think I want to?" His arms tightened about her. "Bethany, my dear one, if there were one place where I knew you would be safe, one person whom I could trust to protect you if I could not, nothing in this life could take you from me. But there is not, so for your own sake you must go back to Barbados."

"I would rather go anywhere than there," she said passionately, without looking up. "You do not know what it has been like, what my life has been these past two years. When Father decided to send me to Jamaica, I was glad to go. I never want to see Barbados again!"

"I know," he said gently, "but this time it will be different. This time the truth will be known."

"Everyone believed me guilty two years ago," she said desolately, "and they are not likely to think differently now."

"They will believe *me*!" Jared's quiet voice was

grim. "And your sister will confess she lied. That I promise you."

"They will believe *you*?" In alarm, Bethany lifted her head to look at him. "Jared, what madness are you planning? You cannot set foot in Barbados."

"I can and I will. Haddon has agreed to set us ashore on a lonely stretch of coast not far from Warrenfield. One of the men once lived in Barbados and knows how this can be done. Pendlecombe and his shipmates will land with us, for they have no real wish to join the Brethren."

"You *are* mad!" she said with conviction. "Pierce would have you made prisoner as soon as he clapped eyes on you, and you would have no hope of escaping again." She broke off, her eyes searching his face, and slowly horror dawned in her own. "You do not intend to try! You would go deliberately to your death."

"Bethany, listen to me!" Jared gripped her by the shoulders and spoke with the utmost earnestness. "The mere fact of my voluntary return when my life is forfeit will lend weight to what I say. By my selfish determination to escape at all costs I brought this trouble upon you, but now, thank God, I am given an opportunity to undo the harm I caused! It is a chance not given to many."

"It is the sort of futile, heroic gesture you once told me you despised," she said hotly. "Throwing your life away to no purpose! Do you think I will let you do it?"

"Do you think you can prevent me?" he countered. "Believe me, love, I have considered well what I do. You say it is to no purpose, but you are wrong. It will be the one action of my life which has any meaning at all."

"I will not listen!" she said in a breaking voice. "Jared, I will go home, I will do anything you ask of me, if only you will abandon this mad intention.

Pendlecombe and the others will take me ashore and
see me safe to Warrenfield or Courtlands. There is no
need even for you to leave the ship."

"There is every need," he replied firmly, "and you
cannot dissuade me from it. What, after all, am I
giving up? A few years at most, for in the Brotherhood men do not grow old. Empty years without you,
knowing that you are still suffering insult and
humiliation because of me. This is the one thing I can
do to make amends."

Bethany pressed her hands to her face, trying to
believe that this was not happening. Happiness had
been so brief, a mere glimpse of all life might have
held, and now it was being taken from her. No, worse
than that! Through all her past tribulations she had
been buoyed up by the thought that Jared was alive
and free, even though they were apart. Now, if he held
to his mad purpose, even that small consolation
would be denied her, and life would have no meaning
at all. She could not bear it. She would want to die,
too.

Six

The *Santa Maria* lay hove-to off the coast of
Barbados, as she had lain throughout the night, and,
a few hundred yards away, the line of the land
showed dark against the brief glory of sunrise. In her
cabin Bethany watched the light grow and brighten,
and as it grew so, too, grew her dread and her despair,
for before the sun set again, Jared would have taken
the final, irrevocable step towards death.

She had failed to turn him from his purpose.
Throughout the long days while the *Santa Maria*
beat back against winds and currents towards
Barbados, she had tried by every means she could
devise to persuade him to change his mind. She had
reasoned with him and pleaded with him; when that
failed she had forced herself to overcome her dread of
the buccaneers sufficiently to approach, with the aid
of John Pendlecombe, the man who was now their
captain, begging him to restrain Jared by force from
landing in Barbados.

Rob Haddon had listened to her civilly enough, but he had refused to interfere. He liked Jared and thought him a fool to throw his life away, but a man's life, after all, was his own, to do with what he willed, and if he wanted to choose the manner of his going from it, that, too, was his own concern. He had agreed to set Jared ashore in Barbados, and that he would do.

Failing to find anywhere the help she sought, Bethany began to grow desperate. Finally, as they drew near to their destination, she resorted to the only other weapon she could think of, the weapon of physical desire, reasoning that if she and Jared became lovers, there could be no question of him sacrificing his life to prove her virtuous. She had used her beauty deliberately, with a shamelessness which, in retrospect, brought a blush to her cheeks, but she had used it in vain. Tempted he might be, but that ruthlessness in him which in the past had enabled him to subordinate all other desires to the determination to escape from slavery, enabled him now to hold fast to a different purpose, to tread unswervingly his chosen path, even though it must lead to his own death, and break Bethany's heart.

She knew that it was his intention to go ashore as soon as it was light, so that the *Santa Maria* could slip quietly away to the safety of the open sea before her presence in those waters was discovered, but she dawdled deliberately over her own preparations. When Jared rapped on her door to ask if she were ready, she had not even begun to dress, and said so with a petulance which sprang from her unutterable wretchedness. There was a pause, and then he said gently:

"Delay can serve no useful purpose, love. I will return in half an hour. Be ready by then."

She heard his footsteps receding through the great cabin, the sound of a closing door, and then silence.

She had been kneeling before the crucifix, praying for a miracle to happen, even at this eleventh hour, to avert the threatened tragedy, but now she rose wearily to her feet. There would be no miracle. In a few hours she would be back at the home which was a home no more, and Jared would be a prisoner.

Listlessly she began to dress. There had been women's garments among the plunder of the *Santa Maria*, and Jared had bargained with his shipmates to obtain some of them for her. Bethany had shrunk from the thought of wearing a dead woman's clothes, but her own had been reduced to such ruin by her adventures that modesty alone obliged her to accept them, and the gown she put on now was a typically Spanish one of black velvet over a silver-embroidered satin petticoat of the same somber color. Like mourning, she thought, and shuddered at the aptness of the reflection.

When Jared returned she was ready, and opened the door in answer to his knock feeling as though it were she who was going to execution. His appearance startled her a little, for hitherto he had been carelessly clad in shirt and breeches, the former open at the throat and with sleeves rolled above the elbow; now he was elegant in crimson brocaded silk, a foam of lace at throat and wrist, boots of fine Spanish leather, and a broad, black hat with a crimson plume. The black leather baldrick supporting his sword was studded and buckled with gold, and he was armed also with a brace of pistols in the leather stole slung, buccaneer-fashion, about his neck. He might be going to imprisonment and death, but, save for the pistols, he was dressed as though for a bridal. She must have betrayed her surprise, for he said lightly:

"Would you have me return as they remember me, in slave's rags or servant's livery? If I appear to have prospered, it will lend even greater weight to what I have to say."

"Jared!" Bethany laid her hands against his chest and raised her face beseechingly towards him. "For the last time, will you not listen to reason? Let me go with Pendlecombe and the others. For my sake, if you will not for your own."

"For your sake, love, and my own, I must go with you. Come, they are waiting for us."

He put his arm about her shoulders to lead her towards the door. For an instant she resisted, then, realizing the futility of it, yielded to the gentle but insistent pressure. Only, as they crossed the cabin, she said with a kind of forlorn desperation:

"Perhaps I can persuade them to be merciful. Father is not without influence, and it must count for something that you saved me and brought me home."

He made no reply. He knew how vain a hope it was, but if it gave her some small measure of comfort to cling to it, he could not bring himself to take it from her. Matthew Court, when he knew the whole truth, might feel more kindly towards him and might even try to intercede for him with the Governor, but Jared cherished no illusions on that score. His escape from Barbados must long since have been reported to the authorities in England, and no colonial Governor, holding his appointment under King James, would dare to show mercy to a fugitive rebel-convict who once already had cheated the gallows by a ruse. Death was waiting for him on the island, and the greatest mercy he could hope for was that it would come quickly, by the rope rather than the whip.

They came on deck to find that four of the survivors of the shipwreck had already been put ashore, and that only John Pendlecombe and one other man remained. The basket had once more been rigged for Bethany; Jared lifted her into it, and the precarious descent was made, less terrifying in a calm sea, but still an ordeal which she was thankful to have behind her. Pendlecombe and his shipmate swarmed down the rope ladder to the boat, and Jared turned to take leave of Rob Haddon, who stood nearby.

"You're still bent on this foolery?" With a jerk of his head the buccaneer captain indicated the waiting boat. "There be time yet to change your mind."

A quick, decisive shake of the head, and an outstretched hand, was the only response. Haddon shrugged, gripped the proffered hand, and then leaned on the bulwarks to watch Jared descend. One might regret a comrade's passing, but one did not mourn for him; death, in the Brotherhood, was too commonplace for that.

The boat grounded among the creaming ripples on the soft white sand, and Pendlecombe and his companion, jumping out, steadied it while Jared carried Bethany ashore. Joining the other men, they watched the boat return to the ship, and the *Santa Maria* prepare to get under way. By the time their own presence on the island was known, she would be safely out of reach.

It took them several hours to reach Warrenfield, for they knew only the general direction in which the plantation lay, and in any event it was impossible to keep to a straight course in the dense, trackless forest. All the men were armed, and two of them, in addition, carried axes with which to clear a path, but to Bethany, hampered by her trailing velvet skirts, it seemed that they toiled through the woods for an eternity. For her sake they rested frequently, and she spun out each halt as long as she could. Her weariness was by no means feigned; she was hot and tired, but most of all she was sick at heart at thought of the inevitable parting from Jared.

At one such halt he threw himself down beside her where she sat leaning wearily against a fallen tree, and looked searchingly and with some concern at her white face.

"Bear up, sweetheart," he said gently. "It cannot be long now before we win out of these infernal woods."

"I would we might never do so!" she murmured unsteadily. "The nearer we get to Warrenfield, the more afraid I am. You do not know Pierce as I do. His temper is so ungovernable at times that he may refuse to listen to anything we say. I wish Courtlands was our destination."

"Warren will listen," Jared assured her with a touch of grimness. "I have the means to ensure it."

She glanced apprehensively at the weapons he bore. "Is that why you go so heavily armed? And why our companions are armed also?"

"Pendlecombe and his shipmates consider themselves in my debt, since I have enabled them to return so promptly to Barbados. Their only alternative was to join the Brethren, and then years might have passed before they made their way home, if, indeed, they ever did so. They will stand by me should need arise."

"I still wish we could go to Courtlands," Bethany said wistfully. "Father would at least give you a hearing, of that I am certain."

Jared did not reply. Bethany was probably right, but she did not know the full extent of what he intended. She thought, for he had deliberately led her to believe it, that it was his intention simply to affirm, as publicly as possible, that she had been grossly slandered by a vindictive servant. This, in fact, was only part of his purpose. He was determined that Esther should admit that she had lied; admit it publicly, if that could be contrived, but certainly to her husband and her father.

When Bethany first told him of her sister's treachery, he had felt a murderous desire to avenge her; to force Esther to admit the truth, and to drive that truth home to Pierce Warren with cold steel.

Even after his decision to return to Barbados, that had still been his intention, but then he realized how much more subtle and complete such a revenge could be. Warren had loved Bethany in his fashion; how bitter, then, for him to know that he had condemned her without cause, on the lying word of the woman who was now his wife. That knowledge, spreading a slow poison which would rankle for years, must surely destroy, for both of them, any contentment they might have found in their marriage. The thought afforded Jared a savage satisfaction.

He looked at Bethany as she sat beside him, one hand tightly clasping his, her eyes closed as she leaned her head wearily on the other. The bright hair, which had been caught up with a Spanish comb of carved ivory, was coming down, curling about her forehead and tumbling on to her shoulders, and her skin seemed whiter than ever by contrast with the rich blackness of the velvet gown. How beautiful she was, even in grief and weariness, and how greatly he loved her! He had not known it was possible to love like this, beyond all thought of self; now, for the first time in his life, he was able to comprehend something of the depth of his mother's feelings for the Earl of St. Orme.

Only Jared himself knew how profoundly he had changed during the past three years, and how much that change was due to Bethany. During those first months of slavery he had plumbed the uttermost depths of desperation, when even the fierce resolve to escape was no more than the last, futile defiance of a spirit on the point of breaking. Then, in the blackest hour of all, in the extreme agony of body and of mind, she had come to him, and drawn him back to life and sanity. Bethany, his savior, his friend, and his love. Now the life she had preserved must be surrendered for her sake, because no lesser price could buy her safety.

Jared did not want to die. Now, more than ever, he wanted to live, though the old, roving life of danger and adventure no longer lured him. He had been heartsick of that even before he knew the source of his disenchantment. He wanted now the things he had hitherto despised; a wife and children, the ties of home and family; but since these were to be denied him, he would give his life in a better cause than the plundering of Spanish ships for personal gain. That he did so of his own free will would undoubtedly command acceptance of what he said; it would be, in effect, the testimony of a dying man.

They resumed their journey, Jared concealing an uneasy suspicion that they were wandering in circles, for surely they should have reached Warrenfield by now. Meeting Pendlecombe's glance, he saw a similar doubt reflected there, but then one of the two sailors leading the little party gave a shout of triumph and pointed ahead, to where, through a gap in the trees, showed a glimpse of cane-fields.

They stumbled out of the forest, and found after a little while one of the broad paths which ran between the blocks of cane, and which would eventually lead them to the plantation buildings. Here the going was easier, and the sailors fell back a little to let Jared and Bethany go ahead. Bethany walked without speaking, clinging tightly to Jared's arm, her whole being crying out in silent protest at the inescapable doom towards which he moved with such steadfast determination. There was no room in her mind now for deluding hopes. He was going to his death, and she knew it as well as he did.

So wrapped in misery was she that several minutes passed before a certain strangeness in the aspect of the cane-fields forced itself upon her, but when it did, she halted and stood looking about her with a puzzled frown. An eerie silence lay over the plantation. There was no movement among the tall rows of cane, no sound of tools or voices or the crack of an overseer's whip; only the hum of insects, and the screech of a bird from the forest behind them. A little shiver of misgiving passed over her, and she looked uneasily at Jared.

"How quiet it is!" she said in a low voice. "Unnaturally quiet!"

He nodded. "So I have been thinking. At this hour everyone should be at work, yet the fields are deserted."

Their companions came up to them, surprised but not yet perturbed, for they were unfamiliar with the daily routine of the cane-fields. Pendlecombe asked curiously:

"Be aught amiss, Mr. Vernon?"

"I am not sure," Jared said slowly. "No work is being done here, but for what reason it is impossible to say. Stay close together as we go on, and keep watch for anything suspicious. We shall have our answer when we reach the plantation house."

They were to have it sooner than that. A minute or two later the path ended in another running at right angles to it, and Bethany and Jared, turning the corner first, almost stumbled over something which lay sprawled in the midst of the way. It was the body of a white man, horribly and savagely mutilated.

Bethany screamed, and Jared, jerking her back with one hand, snatched a pistol from its holster with the other. The other men were as quick as he to draw their weapons, and for a few moments they all stood tense and watchful, ready to resist the attack they expected at any moment to fall upon them. It did not come. The silence, rent for an instant by Bethany's cry, settled again, heavy and menacing, over the

deserted fields, even as the evil clouds of flies,
momentarily disturbed, began to settle again over
the corpse.

Bethany herself, supported now by Jared's left
arm, leaned weakly against him, ashen-faced with
shock. Her eyes were closed, but a horrified whisper
forced its way between her white lips.

"The slaves have risen! Dear God! I feared that one
day he would drive them to it!"

They did not doubt that she was right, for proof of
it was written bloodily at their feet. Pendlecombe
stepped forward and stood looking grimly down at
the dead man, and then pointed to the trampled
ground around the body, where, among the marks of
many bare feet, showed the imprint of a horse's
hooves.

"He were mounted when they pulled him down,"
he said laconically. "Riding for help, belike?"

"Very likely!" Jared's voice was curt. "They must
have sprung out upon him from the other path. A
regiment could conceal itself in this damned cane."

"What should we do, sir?" Pendlecombe asked
uneasily.

"Make for the house. Warren, if he has any sense,
will have gathered there what loyal servants he has,
to defend his family. We can add our number to
theirs, and perhaps, between us, hold off the slaves.
Come! Keep close about Miss Court, and as you love
life, be vigilant!"

With drawn weapons they moved warily forward,
between the walls of sugar-cane where the silence
now was charged with menace. They encountered no
one, living or dead, but after a while they became
aware of a distant uproar of sound, indefinable, yet
ominous in its underlying savagery. It grew louder as
they advanced, and the thought passed uneasily
through Jared's mind that perhaps they came too
late to find shelter at the house. If Warren had been

taken unawares, it might already be in the hands of the rebellious slaves.

They came at last in sight of the roof of it, rising amid the trees of the garden in which it stood. The noise they had heard was louder now, the sound of many clamorous voices, interspersed now and then by shots, but it did not seem to come from the direction of the house. Bethany, more in command of herself now, said unsteadily:

"The mill and storehouses and other buildings are yonder. It sounds as though the fighting is there."

"God grant it remain there, at least until we gain the house," Jared said grimly. "Can you show us the way through the garden?"

She nodded, indicating the path they should follow. In a close-knit group they moved cautiously forward, and now for the first time saw more physical evidence of the uprising, for flowers and shrubs had been trampled underfoot, and the bodies of several slaves, both black and white, lay among the fading blossoms. At length, themselves still sheltered among the trees, Bethany and her companions were able to see that the white-walled house itself appeared to be unscathed.

Its windows were all heavily shuttered and it looked deserted, but Jared had no doubt that their approach was being observed. He had no wish for his party to be mistaken for a group of marauding slaves, so, after another searching look all around, he stepped boldly out into the open and led his companions towards the front door. Immediately a man's voice challenged them from within the house.

"Halt, there! Who are you, and whence do you come?"

"Pierce!" Bethany stepped forward to Jared's side and raised her face towards the blank, blind frontage of the house. "It is Bethany. Please let us in."

There was a moment of stunned silence, and then,

as they moved closer to the door, they heard the sound of chains and bars being hurriedly loosed. The door swung open and Pierce himself appeared on the threshold.

"Bethany?" he said incredulously. "In the name of God, how come you to be *here*? No, no matter! Come within, all of you! Quickly!"

They obeyed, and the servant who had unbarred the door immediately began to secure it again. In the dim candlelight which was the only illumination in the shuttered hall, Pierce gripped Bethany by the shoulders and stared into her face as though still not convinced of her identity.

"What witchcraft brings you here?" he demanded. "We thought you in Jamaica by this time."

"Bethany?" That was Esther's voice, breathlessly echoing her husband's bewilderment. She stood in an open doorway to their right, staring unbelievingly. "It cannot be!"

"Yet it is!" Bethany, more composed than either, moved towards her sister, who shrank back at her approach. "Esther, I am not a ghost. Do not look at me as though I were."

She held out her hand as she spoke, and Esther, almost timidly, put her own into it. Beyond her, in a room more brightly lighted than the entrance hall, Pierce's mother and sisters stood in a staring group. Esther, as though scarcely aware of what she was doing, drew Bethany into the room, and Pierce, motioning Jared to precede him, followed. John Pendlecombe, not waiting for an invitation, led his men after them and stationed himself and them just inside the door.

"I do not understand," Esther was saying. "Bethany, what has happened?"

"The ship sank in a storm two days after we left Barbados."

"Sank?" Esther repeated in a shocked whisper. "What of Captain Mitchell?"

Bethany shook her head. "Only we few survived. Another ship picked us up, and set us ashore this morning a few miles from here."

For the first time Esther became really aware of her sister's companions. She glanced at the little knot of sailors by the door, and then at the elegant gentleman standing beside Pierce a few paces away. From a lean, haughty face, cool gray eyes ironically returned her regard. Her own eyes widened; a hand crept to her throat, and she said in a strangled whisper:

"You!"

Jared swept off his hat and bowed. "Mrs. Warren!" The tone was courteous, but something in his voice and look brought the color flaming into her white face. "Your very obedient servant!"

Pierce looked from one to the other with angry suspicion. The dim light in the hall, and his own overwhelming astonishment at Bethany's arrival, had prevented him from taking a close look at her companion, but now the light was better, and the man's broad hat no longer shadowed his face. Those dark features seemed curiously familiar; after a moment's frowning perplexity, recognition came, and Pierce let fly a thunderous oath.

"Vernon! By God! What treachery is this?"

"No treachery, Warren." Jared's voice was cool and, to Pierce's ears at least, faintly insolent. "I chanced to be aboard the ship which picked up Miss Court and her companions, and therefore have the privilege of bringing her safely home."

"The privilege of being hanged as a runaway slave!" Pierce said contemptuously. "A high price to pay for gallantry, and one no man would risk without some purpose."

"I have a purpose," Jared agreed calmly. "I came back to right a wrong. To prove, to you and to others, that those slanderous tales which linked Bethany Court's name with mine sprang from a deliberate lie."

Esther uttered a little, inarticulate sound of protest and dismay. It was no louder than a whimper, but it caught Pierce's attention sufficiently for him to direct a hard, searching look at her before answering Jared, and made that answer a fraction less scornful than it would otherwise have been.

"So, having discovered that Bethany had been slandered, you came back to disprove it even though you knew that your life would be forfeit! You expect me to believe that?"

"*Because* my life is forfeit," Jared said quietly. "That, Warren, is why you may believe what I say."

There was a pause. The two men, confronting each other like duelists, and the two women who watched them, had forgotten for the present the terror which reigned outside the shuttered house. They were caught up again in the conflict of emotion which, though it had lain dormant for two years, burned as fiercely as ever, and must be resolved now whatever else befell.

"And you will say, I suppose," Pierce remarked after a moment, "that those two servants lied when they said they saw her in your arms that night?"

"No! Neither she nor I deny that one embrace— and that was not the evidence upon which you condemned her. It was not the servants, Warren, who lied."

Bethany made a little, startled gesture of protest which neither Pierce nor Jared heeded. Pierce said in a low, angry voice:

"Damn your impudence! Do you know whom you are accusing?"

"I know!" Jared's voice was still calm; his cool,

compelling gaze held Pierce's steadily. "And I say again, you were told a deliberate lie."

Something in the way he spoke, in his calm, authoritative manner, commanded Pierce's reluctant attention, and slowly, almost unwillingly, he turned his head to look at his wife. After that one, involuntary whimper she had made no sound, but her face was so drained of color that even the lips seemed bloodless, and her eyes, wide and terrified, had the look of a trapped animal's. Already utterly unnerved by the rebellion of the slaves, she had been reduced by this fresh shock to a state wherein she was for the moment incapable of dissembling, incapable of uttering one word in her own defense. Guilt was so plainly written in her face that everyone in the room could read it, and if Jared's words had sown the first seed of doubt in Pierce's mind, Esther's reaction turned it into full-grown certainty.

Staring at him in silent, desperate entreaty, she saw horror and contempt dawning in his eyes. Her own eyes closed, and she swayed as though about to fall, and it was Bethany who started forward to clasp a supporting arm about her waist, for Pierce made no move to assist her.

"A lie!" His voice was low, but indescribably bitter. "A spiteful, deliberate lie—and I, God forgive me, believed it! I even set you in the place which should have been hers!"

He turned abruptly away as though not trusting himself within reach of her, his hand clenched hard on the hilt of his sword as he struggled for self-control. Esther, who at his first words had opened her eyes again, broke away from Bethany to clutch at his arm.

"Pierce, listen to me! It was for your sake! She cares nothing for you. She never has and she never will! Only for him! Pierce...!"

Furiously he wrenched his arm free and thrust her

away, so violently that she staggered and only just saved herself from falling. It was a gesture of repudiation which spoke more clearly than any words, and for a few stunned seconds she could only stare disbelievingly at him. Then she turned on Bethany.

"This is your doing! Why did you have to come back? Why accuse me now, after two years? What can it profit you, today of all days?" She was sobbing, her voice rising hysterically. "No one else will ever know the truth! We are trapped here, and those murderous savages will kill us all. Oh, God have pity on us!"

She flung herself into a chair by the table, burying her face in the crook of one arm and beating her other hand on the polished wood, shrieking incoherently. Pierce did move then. Two quick steps took him to her side; one hand on her shoulder jerked her upright, the other dealt her a stinging slap across the cheek.

"Have done!" he said angrily. "Weeping and wailing will not make amends." He looked across at Bethany. "All is not yet lost! One of my men rode for help. He was to skirt the fields and try to reach the road that way. If he won through...!"

"He did not," Jared interrupted curtly. "We found his body in the fields."

Pierce went white, and his mother gave a little cry of dismay, clasping her two younger daughters in her arms. Jared cast a quick, frowning glance in their direction, and said briskly:

"We can defend the house. It is stoutly built and no doubt well supplied with provisions and arms...!" He broke off, struck by something in Pierce's expression. "Is it not?"

"With provisions," Pierce replied reluctantly, "but not with arms. We were betrayed! This uprising was no sudden thing, but well planned by some of your damned rebels-convict, and other white felons I have purchased since. They subverted even my house-slaves, who intended to admit them to the house just before dawn. Had not my mother's waiting-woman got wind of it and roused me, we should all have been murdered in our beds."

"And the weapons?" Jared demanded.

Pierce shook his head. "Already stolen to arm the uprising, leaving only my personal arms. One or two of our oldest slaves remain loyal—the others fled when their treachery was discovered. We were in time to bar the doors before their fellows joined them, and, my head overseer and one or two of his men firing on them from the rear as I did so from the house, they took flight. But they will return."

"Yes," Jared agreed grimly. "they will return. Finding themselves thwarted here, their next thought will have been food and drink. Especially drink! They must have seized the stores by now, but when they have had their fill of looting where there is none to stay them, they will attack again." He looked at Pierce with a frown. "How many men have you?"

"A mere half-dozen, including myself. That is why I dared send no more than one to raise the alarm."

"Another must go now," Jared said curtly. "Our coming had doubled the number of defenders, and we are all armed, but even a dozen will not be able to hold the house indefinitely. Help *must* be fetched from Bridgetown."

"Best to go now, then, sir." John Pendlecombe spoke for the first time. "Afore them devils drinks enough heart into themselves to come at us again. We saw none on 'em as we came here, so a man'd mebbe have a chance to get away afore they knows it."

"Unlikely, my friend!" Jared said dryly. "Men capable of planning an uprising as well as Warren says this was planned will not neglect to set a watch of some kind, though one might contrive to evade it in the fields if one went on foot."

"It is not in the fields that they will keep watch,"

Bethany said suddenly. "There is only one road from Warrenfield to Bridgetown—that which goes by way of Courtlands. If that is barred, the only other way is through the woods."

"Small chance of summoning help in time by way of the forest," Jared said grimly. "The road it must be, then, and the sooner the better."

"How do us decide who shall go?" Pendlecombe asked practically. "Draw lots?"

"No." Jared removed the stole bearing his pistols, and his sword and sword-belt, and laid them on the table at which Esther still sat, her face hidden in her hands. "It must be he who has the greatest chance of winning through. I will go."

Bethany uttered a little sound of anguished protest, hastily stifled, and Pierce said with a sneer:

"You have no small conceit of yourself, Vernon, but you will not save your neck by playing the hero."

He knew that the taunt was unworthy, but could not resist uttering it. Jared flashed him a look of contempt.

"My chance is greatest because I, too, have been a slave, and therefore, more than any man here, can hope to guess how they will act." He stripped off his coat and dropped it across a chair. "Let us hope also that there is some truth in the old adage that dog does not eat dog."

"Do you suppose that if they discover you, they will give you time to tell them of your slavery?"

"There will be no need." Jared's satin waistcoat followed the coat, and then he dragged off the ruffled shirt, baring his sunburned, powerfully muscled torso and the ugly grid of scars across his back. "Like them, I bear the badge of it." He looked at Bethany and smiled faintly. "I never thought the day would come when I would be grateful for that flogging."

She could not respond to the implicit appeal to her

courage; the fate of the earlier messenger was too horribly vivid in her mind, and every instinct rebelled at seeing Jared go from her now. If these were to be the last few hours of life, then they ought to spend them together. Yet she knew it would be useless to protest. By his very nature he was incapable of waiting passively for the blow to fall; as long as there was a chance, however slight, he must take it, in the hope of saving them all.

Jared picked up his sword, held it for a moment and then laid it again on the table. "That will be more hindrance than help," he remarked. "Pistols will serve me better, and a knife. Pendlecombe, let me have yours."

Pendlecombe promptly handed over the formidable blade, and Jared strapped the sheath to his belt. Then, taking up the pistols, thrust one of those into his belt also, but turned to Bethany and put the other into her hand.

"Keep that," he said in a low voice. "I pray to God that you will have no cause to use it, but if you must...!"

She took the weapon without argument, but laid it aside and, regardless of those about them, cast herself into his arms. She could not speak, knowing that if she did, it would be to distress him with entreaties to stay, but she tried to convey, by that last, long kiss, everything of love and faith for which no words seemed adequate. For a few timeless seconds the world was theirs alone, and then he raised his head, looked for a moment into her eyes, and then put her from him and went quickly from the room.

Pierce followed him into the hall, there was a curt, low-voiced exchange, and then the sound of the door being unbarred. A few tense moments of silence followed, during which it was easy to picture the two men looking searchingly about the garden, and then the rattle of bolts and chains again and Pierce came slowly back into the room.

Bethany picked up the garments Jared had discarded and folded them neatly, carefully smoothing the fine stuff with steady hands. She placed sword and swordbelt on top, and went to lay them all in a chest in the far corner of the room. It was an act of faith, a silent avowal of her belief that he would survive to wear them again.

Pierce watched Bethany with tormented eyes, and then swung to face John Pendlecombe and the other sailors. "You will be glad of food and drink," he said abruptly. "My own men are keeping watch, and you had best take a meal while you may." He glanced at his mother. "Madam, will you see to it?"

Mrs. Warren looked startled, cast an involuntary glance at Esther, and then murmured something indistinguishable and signed to the men to follow her. Esther herself, who had looked up at Pierce's first words, sat silent and humiliated as they trooped out, for by that brief request to his mother Pierce had tacitly restored her to the place of mistress of the house, which she had relinquished by custom at the time of his marriage.

He did not look at Esther. His attention had returned at once to Bethany, and now he went across to her where she still stood by the chest, her head bowed, either oblivious of or indifferent to what was happening.

"Bethany, I must talk to you," he said desperately. "Alone!"

She raised her head, but for a second or two the blue eyes were blank and unseeing, seeming to look beyond him as though he did not exist. Familiar jealousy ran through him like fire, for he knew that in heart and mind and spirit she was following Jared Vernon on his perilous mission, and that nothing else could hold any real importance for her. Then her gaze focused upon him, and she nodded.

"Yes," she said with a sigh, "we must talk. There are many things which must be explained."

He turned to his wife. "Go up to the nursery. Take my sisters with you."

For a moment it seemed that she would defy him, but the habit of obedience was too strong. The three girls were already moving meekly towards the door; Esther got slowly to her feet and, with a look of bitter resentment at her sister, reluctantly followed. As the door closed behind them, Pierce said in the same desperate tone:

"In God's name, Bethany! Why did you not tell me she was lying?"

"Why did you not ask me?" she countered quietly. "Why accept another's word that I was guilty, even if that other were my sister?"

"Because she *is* your sister! How could I, or anyone, suppose that Esther—*Esther*—would lie about such a thing?"

"You could more readily suppose that I had betrayed you?" Bethany moved to the table and sat down; her voice was calm, as though they were discussing some other person. "The fault was not wholly Esther's, Pierce! You never really trusted me."

"I think it was my own good fortune I could not trust," he said wretchedly. "We were betrothed, but that was our fathers' doing and I lived in constant dread that you secretly preferred some other man. When our marriage had to be delayed you seemed to grow more and more aloof, and I saw how you favored Vernon, and I was bitterly jealous. Jealous of a slave! Yet I swear to you, Bethany, that when I rode to Courtlands that day, I never really believed that you had been false to me. I had no doubt that you had helped him to escape, and I was furious with you for provoking such a scandal, but had it not been for Esther ... !" He broke off, his anger and bitterness too great for words, and struck the table with his clenched fist. "I will never forgive her for coming between us!"

"It was not Esther who came between us," Bethany said calmly. "What she did simply prevented our marriage. That is what you must try to understand. Had you married me, Pierce, I would have been a loyal wife to you, but I could never have loved you. Esther does. That is why she did what she did."

"You loved me once," he said jealously. "Before that damned rebel came on the scene."

She shook her head. "I held you in deep affection, Pierce. We grew up together knowing that we were to be married, and I accepted that as natural and right. I did not then know the reality of love."

"But now you do? You have found that reality with Vernon?"

"Yes," she said simply, "and because of it I can understand Esther. Understand and forgive, as I hope you will do."

There was no need, she thought, to tell him that Esther's motive had been more complex than the straightforward jealousy of a woman in love with her sister's future husband; that she cherished a hatred which reached back into childhood and was never likely to be satisfied while life endured. If there were to be any hope of future amity between them— supposing that they escaped from the present perilous situation—he must somehow be reconciled to his marriage. Bethany had not known what Jared intended; she knew he had done it for her sake and could not blame him; but she knew, too, that she must try to prevent it from doing irreparable harm.

"You can forgive?" Pierce said incredulously.

"Even the undeserved shame and disgrace you have had to endure?"

"What does that matter now?" she asked impatiently. "We stand in the very shadow of death, and even if help reaches us in time, life for me can no longer hold any hope of happiness. What use, then, in brooding vengefully over what is past? The one thought which now possesses my mind is that, because of me, Jared has returned here to his death."

So self-centered was he that until that moment, this had not occurred to him. That death in one form or another waited in Barbados for Jared Vernon had caused him to feel only satisfaction, but now, for the first time, he realized what this must mean to Bethany. From that, curiosity was born, and he was moved at last to inquire how such a situation had come about.

Briefly she told him, since it could not matter now if Jared were known for a buccaneer. Pierce listened without comment, masking whatever emotion the story aroused in him, but when she paused he said with some perplexity:

"This I cannot understand. You were free, you were together, you say you love one another. You could have settled anywhere, with none to stay you. Why then, in the fiend's name, did you come back to Barbados?"

Bethany, explaining Jared's reasons for bringing her home, had little hope of Pierce understanding or agreeing with them, and was not surprised when, at the end, he shook his head in bewilderment.

"If this be love, to sign his own death-warrant and thus inflict bitter sorrow upon you, then it is something I cannot comprehend. Had I been in his place I would have thanked God for bringing you to me, nor questioned the Divine working of Providence."

It was pointless to pursue the subject. Bethany

said with a sigh: "But return we did, and, for good or
ill, you know the truth. Yet if you allow it to turn you
against Esther, who loves you as I never could; if you
let it poison the life you must share with her, it will be
yet another heavy load of sorrow and regret for me to
bear. Pierce, I entreat you, make your peace with
her!"

"That is easier said than done," he replied
ungraciously. "Do you suppose I can soon forget her
treachery, her betrayal of you?"

"Must we take always the easy road? If we survive
this day, you and Esther will face a lifetime together,
and you will suffer as much as she if you let it hold
nothing but bitterness and resentment. For your own
sake as much as for hers, do not allow that to
happen."

"I suppose there is truth in what you say," he
agreed reluctantly. "We are wed, and nothing can be
done to alter that, no matter how much I may wish it
otherwise. It shall be known, though, how she lied
about you and Vernon. She shall not escape that!"

"But you will endeavour not to hold it against her?
Promise me that!"

"I'll endeavor it, since *you* ask it of me."

"And you will go to her now, and set her mind at
rest? We cannot tell what time is left to us."

"If that is what you want me to do, I will, though
God knows I have little heart for it!" He leaned one
hand on the table, the other on the back of her chair,
looking searchingly into her face. "You say you
forgive Esther, but can you ever forgive me? I know
full well that if I had not turned from you the gossip
concerning you and Vernon would soon have been
forgotten."

"I forgave you, Pierce, long since. I would have
done you a far worse wrong than you did me, if I had
married you loving Jared as I do."

"Would that you could have loved me so," he said

bitterly. "I still think Vernon was mad to bring you back. For your sake, if for no other reason, he should have sought to preserve his life, not cast it away."

"Perhaps, if he wins through to Courtlands to summon help, the Governor may show him mercy ... !" Bethany's words trailed into silence as she saw the pity in Pierce's eyes. "You do not think so?"

He shook his head. "It would be cruel to delude you with a hope which, in your heart, you already know to be false. However much inclined to leniency His Excellency might feel, Vernon stands convicted of high treason as well as being a runaway slave, and he would not dare to pardon him. At the very least, Vernon would certainly be sentenced to a flogging, and to return to the plantation if he survived it. Would that be any mercy at all?"

Bethany shuddered. "No," she whispered, "it would be the greater cruelty. He could not endure slavery again."

She rested her elbows on the table and bowed her face on her hands, overwhelmed at last by the despair which, while they talked, she had managed to hold at bay. This was the end. Even if she saw Jared again, it would be as a prisoner under sentence of death; and if such a meeting did take place, it would mean that the present danger had been escaped and that she was under sentence, too. Sentenced to live on alone with only bitter-sweet memories and vain regrets.

The attack, when it came, was sudden and fierce. For some time the watchers in the house had seen slaves moving furtively among such shelter as the garden offered, and though the temptation to fire upon the skulking figures had been strong, they forced themselves to resist it. Their supply of powder and shot was perilously small, and to open fire might well provoke a concerted attack.

That the slaves were working themselves up to the point of assaulting the house was plain. The distant commotion which, when Bethany and her companions arrived, had held a note of jubilation, had drawn nearer and changed in character. As Jared, from his own experience, had been able to guess, the slaves, after subsisting for months and years at starvation level, had easily been diverted from their first, bloody purpose by the opportunity to raid the stores of food, and of the rum distilled from the sugar-cane they had been enslaved to cultivate. The fierce spirit, aptly nicknamed "kill-devil," had done its deadly work, adding drunkenness to the hatred and the despairing lust for vengeance out of which the uprising had sprung.

Having plundered, they burned. The sugar-mill and other buildings, the stockade and the whipping-post, even the wretched huts which had sheltered them. The Negroes, many of them newly brought from Africa, were whipping themselves to a frenzy as they had done for tribal wars in their native land, and the savage, primitive rhythm of their war-chant beat terrifyingly against the shuttered windows of the house. Those who waited within could feel the mounting tension, the rising wave of fury which must break soon in violence.

Pierce sent the women to wait in the nursery on the upper floor, where, if the slaves succeeded in breaching the defenses of the house, it would be easier for him and the other men to protect them. They gathered there almost in silence; Esther and Bethany; Mrs. Warren with her three daughters; Tabitha, whom Mr. Court had sent to Warrenfield before Esther's baby was born; and the waiting-woman, Hepzibah, who had first raised the alarm.

The chanting and yelling outside, which had been growing ever louder, reached an unbearable pitch of excitement, and then to the waiting, listening women it seemed as though all hell broke loose. The slaves launched themselves at the house from every side, faltered and gave ground before the unexpected vigor of its defense, then rallied and came on again. The noise was indescribable, shouts, screams and the rattle of musketry combining in one fiendish uproar. The baby woke and began to cry, Pierce's youngest sister burst into tears also, and Hepzibah, crouched in a corner of the room, flung her apron over her head and rocked to and fro, moaning with terror.

Mrs. Warren huddled her daughters about her, Tabitha was helping Esther to soothe the frightened baby, but Bethany went to the window and set her eye to the spy-hole in one of the shutters. She could see only a little of the scene below, but it was enough to convince her that unless help came soon, they were all doomed. A dozen men, had they been well provided with weapons and ammunition, could have held the stoutly built house indefinitely, but only with fire-arms could the slaves be held off. Once the powder and shot was exhausted there would be no way of preventing the attackers from breaking down the door, and once within they must prevail by sheer weight of numbers. Pierce had complied with the law in having the required number of white servants in proportion to black, but it was some of these who had planned and led the uprising. They were desperate men with nothing to lose save lives grown intolerable, and their only purpose was to wreak a terrible vengeance before they died.

Several hours had passed since Jared's departure. If he had won through to Courtlands with his warning, Bethany knew that her father would have wasted no time in raising the alarm, and help might even now be on its way. If it were not...! She turned away from the scene of carnage below, and looked instead at the pistol Jared had given her before he left. She knew that he had intended her to use it upon herself, rather than fall alive into the hands of the maddened slaves.

The noise of battle continued with unabated vigor, but gradually Bethany became aware of a subtle change in its composition. The shots from within the house were growing fewer, until only an occasional report rang out, though those outside the house did not slacken. She glanced at her companions, and, meeting Mrs. Warren's frightened gaze across the candle-lit room, knew that Pierce's mother, at least, had realized the significance of the change.

Before long the others could remain in ignorance of it no more, for the sound of heavy, regular blows against the front door came distinctly to their ears, indicating that the attackers, no longer under fire from the house, had improvised some kind of battering-ram. Steady and threatening, the sound went on and on, insistent as the thudding of their own frightened hearts.

There were other sounds within the house, the scraping and bumping of heavy furniture being shifted to reinforce the door, and then similar noises closer at hand on the upper floor. Bethany went out, and found some of the men dragging furniture from the other rooms to barricade the head of the stairs. John Pendlecombe, grim-faced, was directing their labors.

"The door below won't hold 'em much longer, mistress," he said laconically, seeing her dismayed look. "Mr. Warren bade us build a second barricade here. 'Twill win us a few minutes more."

A few minutes more of agonized waiting for the rescue which might not come. Bethany thrust the thought firmly from her mind.

"There are backstairs also," she said in a low voice. "The slaves who worked in the house will know of them."

"Aye, Mr. Warren told us. We've built another barrier there."

From below came a crash of splintering wood, a yell of triumph from the attackers, and then the assault on the door was resumed with added vigor. Bethany, craning on tiptoe to see through the narrow gap still open in the barricade, heard Pierce order his companions below to fall back to the upper floor, but since the staircase rose in three flights, each at right angles to the next, she could not see down the hall. Footsteps pounded on the stairs and the men came hurrying into view, as another rending crash sounded from below.

Pierce himself followed last of all, when those before him were already struggling through the gap on to the upper landing. He was halfway up the second flight when a shot rang out. He jerked to a halt, spun half round and dropped, sliding down two or three of the stairs he had just mounted. The man in front of him, already halfway through the barricade, drew back and, bending low to get what shelter he could from the ornately carved balustrade, returned to Pierce, half-dragged, half-carried him up the remaining flight and thrust him into the hands outstretched to help him through to the meager protection of the landing.

While they were hurriedly blocking the gap, Bethany bent over Pierce, huddled now on the floor behind the barricade. His face was gray, and there was a spreading stain of blood on his coat. She called to one of the old house-slaves who had remained loyal.

"Take your master into the nursery," she said briefly, and without waiting to see the order obeyed flew into the nearest ransacked bedchamber to snatch up pillows and bed-linen.

She heard Esther scream as Pierce was helped into

the room, and when Bethany herself re-entered the nursery, her sister was on her knees beside her husband, supporting him in her arms. His eyes were closed, and his head lolled helplessly against her breast.

Bethany beckoned Tabitha, and between them, with Mrs. Warren's help, they got pillows beneath him and ripped open his clothing to expose the ugly wound in his right side. The musket-ball had gone deep, and all they could hope to do was staunch the bleeding and do what little they could to ease his pain. Bethany, tearing a sheet into strips to serve as bandages, saw Tabitha shaking her head, and wondered grimly whether, even if rescue came in time to save the rest of them, it would be in time now to save Pierce.

If it were to come at all, she thought, it must come soon. A terrific crash from below had indicated that the first barrier had given way, and now the noise of battle sounded nearer at hand, as the remaining defenders sought to hold the second. That they were able to do so at all was due wholly to the fact that, even on the main staircase, the attackers could only come at them a few at a time, but in the end the appallingly heavy odds against them must prevail.

Pierce, still clasped in Esther's arms, lay inert while they dressed the wound, but when it was done, and a blanket wrapped about him, consciousness unexpectedly returned. He groaned and opened his eyes, looking dazedly at the anxious faces of his wife and mother as they bent over him. Then the clouded gaze cleared and he said in a hoarse whisper:

"Bethany! Where is Bethany?"

She had been standing just out of his range of vision, but after an instant's hesitation she moved closer and bent over him, saying in a calm voice:

"I am here, Pierce. Lie still and save your strength."

Instead of obeying, he stretched out a wavering hand towards her, and after another fractional pause she took it in her own. His fingers closed weakly on hers.

"Help will not come!" His feeble voice held a note of the utmost anguish. "And I can no longer protect you. Oh, God! If only you were safe elsewhere!"

Involuntarily Bethany's dismayed glance lifted to her sister's face. Esther was deathly pale, and if Bethany had ever wished to see her punished, that wish was gratified now. In Esther's eyes was the knowledge of utter defeat. She was Pierce's wife, she had borne his son, but it was her sister he still loved. In the present extreme of danger he could think of no one else, and, weak and wounded, was no longer capable of pretense, but spoke with complete honesty, straight from the heart.

His weak clasp on Bethany's hand relaxed, and his eyes closed as he slid back into unconsciousness. Across his still figure the two sisters looked at one another.

"Are you satisfied?" Esther's low voice was indescribably bitter. "You have always taken, as of right, everything I ever valued."

Bethany stretched out her hand. "Esther, in pity's name! Death is very close for all of us, so let there be an end of all hatred and jealousy between you and me."

"Easy to say, when you have all and I nothing!" Esther struck the proffered hand violently aside. "Death itself will not change my feelings towards you!"

Bethany straightened up and moved quickly away, pierced by an anguish which had nothing to do with Esther's refusal to be reconciled. "You have all," her sister had said, yet what, after all, did she have? Not even the bitter consolation of being with her love at the last.

Where was he now? Had he won through to
Courtlands and so to imprisonment, or did he lie
somewhere out in the fields, murdered as that other
man had been murdered? She would never know. She
took up the pistol he had given her, guessing, from
the sound of the desperate, hand-to-hand fighting at
the staircasehead, that very soon now she would
have to find the resolution to use it.

The sudden, fierce rattle of musketry from the
garden did not at first convey any message to her
mind; it needed the noise of a second volley to rouse
her to half-frightened, half-incredulous hope, and
send her rushing to the spy-hole in the shutter.
Figures were moving among the trees and shrubs
below, she glimpsed mounted men, and the scarlet
coats of the militia, and saw the slaves who had been
attacking and plundering the house fleeing in panic,
or making a desperate stand against this new and
unexpected assault. With tears of relief stinging her
eyes, she spun round to face the room.

"We are saved! Help has come from Bridgetown!"

They stared at her, seemingly unable to grasp the
meaning of what she had said. Then Pierce's eldest
sister, Mary, sprang to the window in her turn.

"It is true! I can see them! Many of them!"

She flung her arms round her younger sisters and
they clung together, sobbing with relief, while their
mother, still kneeling at Pierce's side, began to
murmur a prayer of thanksgiving. Bethany stood,
gripping the pistol, leaning against the wall beside
the shuttered window, savoring a relief so profound
that it was almost too much to bear. Jared was alive.
Imprisonment, trial, even the certainty of his conviction, faded for the moment into insignificance beside
that glad realization.

Her unalloyed relief endured for a few moments
only, and then alarm forced its way in again. The
sounds of conflict at the head of the staircase had not

diminished; rather did they seem to be increasing in volume, as though the defenders had been obliged to retreat. A sudden resounding crash added force to the impression, and Bethany went quickly to the door and opened it a crack.

What she saw filled her with dismay. With the rescuers advancing through the garden, the majority of the slaves had either fled or turned to face them, but those leading the assault on the stairs were the most hardy and desperate of them all, and, being certain of death in any event, possessed the fearlessness of complete despair. Trapped they might be, but they were determined to wreak a terrible vengeance on their master and his womenfolk. Part of the barricade had already fallen, and even as Bethany watched, another portion came crashing down.

She shut the door and looked for key or bolt which might serve to win a few moments' delay, but there was neither. Another crash, and the clash of steel drawing nearer. She backed away, still watching the door, her heart thudding so violently with fear that it felt as though it must choke her.

There was a sudden flurry of movement outside, a heavy thud, and then the door crashed back on its hinges to reveal a huge Negro, his black skin glistening with sweat and streaked with blood. His face was distorted with fury, the light of madness was in his eyes, and, in his hand, a great cane-knife, dripping red. For an instant he paused in the doorway, glaring about the room, and then his glance alighted on Pierce, ashen-faced and still, clasped in the arms of his kneeling wife. A savage cry of triumph broke from the slave's lips, and he sprang forward with the razor-sharp blade upraised.

Bethany's pistol cracked, with a dart of flame as vicious as a snake's tongue, and a report deafening in the confined space of the shuttered room. The slave was barely two paces from her when she fired, and at

that close range even a trembling and inexperienced
hand could not aim amiss. The Negro stiffened as
though he had been jerked off his feet by some
invisible force and then pitched to the floor, the
blood-strained machete falling from his hand to skid
and slide across the polished boards to Esther's side.
One of the girls shrieked, and the baby, clasped in
Tabitha's arms, began to yell again, more lustily
than before.

Bethany stood, white-faced and horror-stricken,
staring down at the corpse at her feet. At that
murderously close range the shot had wrought
horrible havoc, and, as realization of what she had
done dawned upon her, she cast the pistol from her
with a gesture of loathing and pressed both hands to
her cheeks. A scream was rising in her throat and she
choked it frantically back, knowing that if once she
allowed herself to utter it, she would be unable to stop.

They were still fighting in the corridor outside the
nursery, but now another man hacked his way
through the press of struggling figures to the open
door and halted there, checked for a moment by what
he saw. Then he strode forward, stepping over the
slave's body, and caught Bethany up in his arms. She
looked up incredulously into Jared's beloved face,
and then with a great sob buried her own face against
him, weeping uncontrollably.

Other men followed him into the room, but she was
scarcely aware of them, and totally uncaring. The
terrors and tensions of the day, the culminating
horror of taking a human life, had wrought her to a
pitch very close to breaking-point, and only the fact
of Jared's presence, when she had imagined him
already a prisoner, kept her from complete collapse.
Even when her father thrust his way into the room
she was unaware of it. Matthew Court took a step
towards her, hesitated for a moment while his glance

met Jared's above her head, and then, as though thinking better of it, turned instead towards Esther, leaving Jared and Bethany together.

Seven

Presently, when the violence of her weeping had abated a little, it occurred to her to question the miracle of his presence, when she had expected him to be thrown immediately into prison. By that time he had carried her to the far side of the room, away from the body of the man she had killed, and set her on her feet again with her back to the sprawling corpse. He looked tenderly down at her tear-streaked face.

"The Governor agreed to accept my parole until we knew the outcome of this business, for it was necessary to muster as many men as we could in the shortest possible time. I have your father, though, to thank for the fact that His Excellency agreed to my request."

"Father?" Bethany murmured in bewilderment.

"He realized, I think, that I would have run mad, mewed up in gaol and unable to lift a finger to aid you, not even knowing whether you were alive or dead." His arms tightened about her; his voice was rough and shaken with emotion. "All the while, that dread tormented me. That we might come too late. When we sighted the house, and found that the slaves had already broken into it...!"

He stopped abruptly, unable to express in words the horror of that moment, the appalling conviction that nothing remained but to avenge her death; a conviction which had not been entirely dispelled until he forced his way into this room and saw her standing there with the Negro's body at her feet. Even now the narrowness of her escape made him feel sick with shock.

"God is merciful," she whispered. "He has brought us both safely through this day's perils; mine here, and yours in your bid to summon help. Oh, Jared, I prayed for you, but it seemed scarcely possible that you could evade all the slaves."

"They were watching the road, as you guessed they would, but I contrived to pass. Your prayers were a potent shield, love!"

Later she was to discover that he had killed three of the slaves who tried to stop him, and had covered the distance to Courtlands in an unbelievably short time, a feat which was to be remembered in Barbados for a long while to come. The prompt crushing of the uprising which, left unchecked, might well have spread like wildfire to engulf the whole colony, was due entirely to him, and he had borne a major part, too, in the counter-attack by which this had been accomplished. He had placed everyone, from the Governor down, under the deepest obligation, yet he was a man marked for death by due process of the Law, and not even his great service to the colony could outweigh that.

The last of the slaves fighting in the house had now been killed or had surrendered, and Mr. Court sent a man in haste to summon the surgeon who had come with the rescuers from Bridgetown. Meanwhile

Tabitha and Hepzibah did what they could to set one of the bedchambers to rights, and to this Pierce was presently carried. Esther and Mrs. Warren went with him, and before long Bethany found herself alone with Pierce's sisters and the wailing infant, for Jared had gone to help round up such slaves as could be found, and Mr. Court accompanied the surgeon to Pierce's room.

She was so tired that she scarcely knew what she was doing, and racked again by the anguish on Jared's behalf which had returned hard upon the heels of her first relief. She left the three girls to attend to the baby, and dropped wearily into a chair, knowing that her courage and her endurance alike were at en end. An eternity seemed to have passed since from her cabin aboard the *Santa Maria* she had watched the dawn of this eventful day brighten across the sky; now there was no longer anything for which to strive, for nothing she did could change the course of events, and, with the end of effort, exhaustion overcame her.

She had intended only to rest for a few minutes, but she must have fallen asleep, for when she opened her eyes again Jared was standing before her, dressed once more in the courtly attire he had worn that morning. As she looked blankly up at him, he said quietly:

"I must go now, Bethany. All is quiet here, and the slaves can do no further harm."

"Go?" She spoke dazedly, groping for comprehension, her mind still drugged with weariness. "Go where?"

"Back to Bridgetown, to yield up my parole. Captain Maynard goes to report to His Excellency, and I ride with him."

She understood then, and dismay brought her up out of the chair and into his arms. Useless to plead or argue; they had both known, from the moment the

return to Barbados was decided upon, that it must
lead inevitably to this. There was no more to be said;
only a broken murmur of farewell, a last embrace,
and then he was gone. Bethany stood rigid and
unmoving, her hands tightly gripped together. She
did not weep, as she had wept earlier with shock and
relief. This anguish went deeper, too deep to find
expression in tears; too deep for anything but a numb
and frozen despair.

A hand touched her shoulder, and slowly, as
though she were once more awakening from sleep,
she looked up into her father's face. It was a moment
or two before she realized that, for the first time in two
years, there was no condemnation in his eyes. That
he was looking at her as he used to look before
Esther's lies had come between them, and in anger
and shame at her supposed disgrace he had turned
against her. Yet there was something else, too;
something other than love and pity; a hint of
entreaty.

"Vernon told me the truth before we rode hither,"
he said in a low voice, "and now Mrs. Warren
confirms that Esther confessed that she lied. I
wronged you bitterly, my child! I should have known
better."

"You were not to blame, sir," Bethany said
wearily. A few weeks ago she would have given the
world to hear him admit his mistake, but now it
scarcely seemed to matter. "Why should you, more
than anyone else, doubt Esther's word?"

"Because I know her, and you, better than most. I
should have known that, whatever you had done, you
would not try to deceive me. Even had her charge
been true, you would not have sought to conceal the
fact."

"No," she said in an odd, reflective tone, "for I
would have felt no cause for shame. I love Jared, but
he has never been my lover, then or now." Then the

icy, unnatural composure cracked; her lips trembled, the blue eyes darkened with pain. "Oh, Father, help us! Find a way to save him!"

"Would that I could, child!" Mr. Court put his arms round her as she buried her face against his shoulder. "We all owe him a debt of gratitude this day." He looked down at her, filled with love and compassion and remorse that he had no power to express in words. "Tomorrow we will return to Courtlands. I will see His Excellency, but, Bethany, my child, do not set your hopes too high."

It was as well that Mr. Court uttered that warning, and that Bethany heeded it, for the Governor, when approached, admitted reluctantly that he could do nothing. His sympathy Jared undoubtedly had, and his gratitude, just as he had the gratitude of everyone in Bridgetown, but though the colonists of Barbados were well aware of the debt they owed Jared Vernon, it was not to be supposed that the authorities in England would appreciate it. In Barbados the threat of a servile uprising was a constant nightmare, and yesterday that nightmare had almost become reality. In England, half the world away, echoes of that terror would sound but faintly, and King James and his Council remember only that the man who had averted disaster was himself a fugitive slave, a rebel-convict already condemned for high treason. His Excellency would have liked nothing better than to issue a pardon, but that he dare not do.

So Jared remained in prison, awaiting his trial, and though Bethany was allowed to visit him, and found him so comfortably housed that her more immediate and trivial anxieties on his behalf were allayed, such visits were a torment rather than a comfort to either of them. They tried, each for the other's sake, to make a pretense of keeping up their spirits, but it was a pretense which grew more difficult with each day that passed.

Bethany had expected and feared that he would be brought to trial almost at once, but it seemed that an unexpected obstacle had arisen, and the Governor told Matthew Court that he doubted whether a court could be found in the island which would convict Vernon. Popular feeling was wholeheartedly on his side. Springing from appreciation of the service he had rendered, nourished by the story of the reason for his return, which now was common knowledge, it was a tide running so strongly in his favor that the Governor and his advisers were reluctant to risk opposing it.

Just how the facts had become known, Bethany was not sure. Not from Pierce, now beginning to recover from his wound but still helpless at Warrenfield; certainly not from Esther, who, though she knew she had betrayed herself, now preserved a sullen silence. Bethany suspected Mary Warren, who was devoted to her and had bitterly resented Pierce's marriage to Esther. Mary and the two other Warren girls were staying at Courtlands, and there had been a constant stream of visitors there, all eager to see for themselves that Bethany Court really had come home, and curious to discover the how and the why of her return. The story, somewhat exaggerated but nevertheless true in all its essentials, had caught people's imagination, and they were as ready now to sympathize with Bethany as they had been, two years before, to condemn her.

Stalemate, it seemed, had been reached, and Mr. Court, watching Bethany with loving concern, wondered anxiously how long she would be able to endure the appalling strain. On the surface she was calm enough, but there were shadows like bruises beneath her eyes, and in the eyes themselves a look sometimes of utter desperation.

So matters stood on the day when a message from the Governor arrived at Courtlands, requesting Mr. Court and Bethany to present themselves without delay at Government House. Both leapt immediately to the conclusion that the summons heralded some move to bring Jared to trial at last, and as they rode down towards the town Bethany felt that she was moving in an evil dream. She had thought that nothing could be worse than waiting for the blow to fall, but now that it was falling at last she would have given anything to turn back the clock.

This was the road she had so often ridden with Jared in the days when he was her servant, and every yard of it evoked memories which today were more poignant and heart-breaking than ever before. Here, the first time he attended her, she had rebuked him for his misplaced gallantry; here Pierce had surprised them riding side by side and so absorbed they never even noticed his approach; this turn of the road offered the first glimpse of the harbor, where the Dutch brig had once lain but where, today, a ship newly arrived from England rode at anchor in the same place.

When they reached Government House and entered its spacious entrance hall, they found Jared himself there, under the escort of a sergeant and two privates of the militia. They went to join him, and Mr. Court asked in a low voice:

"What mean this summons, Vernon? Do you know?"

Jared shook his head, taking Bethany's hand and lifting it to his lips. "I know no more than you do, sir, and neither do these fellows. They were simply ordered to bring me here, nor given any reason why."

He looked at Bethany, his gaze lingering like a caress on her pale face, seeing, beneath the desperate calm and the determined valor, the anguish she might contrive to hide from others but not from him, for it was but a reflection of the anguish in his own heart. Racked by love and pity, he found himself hoping for her sake that the Governor's summons foreshadowed an early end to this intolerable waiting. There was no hope of pardon; since death must come, in God's name let it come soon. The agony she suffered then would be sharp, like a surgeon's knife probing a festering wound, but once the pain and the shock were over, time's slow, inevitable process of healing would begin.

After a few minutes' delay they were ushered into the Governor's presence. Jared's escort being left behind. They found His Excellency alone, at a table strewn with documents, from which he rose at once to greet them, and to hand Bethany to a chair. Jared, watching him, thought that he could detect some strong emotion beneath the formal manner, though what it was he could not guess.

"I have summoned you here, Vernon," His Excellency said abruptly, "because I have just received tidings which, while affecting profoundly all those who owe allegiance to the English Crown, hold for you an even greater and more personal significance. A ship has arrived from England, bearing news of vast changes there." He paused, looking from one to the other. "Early last November, at the invitation of the representatives of the English people, William of Orange landed at Torbay with a considerable force. Throughout the country he was welcomed, and hailed as a deliverer. By the middle of December, King James, with the Queen and the infant Prince, and certain gentlemen closest to him in his counsels, had fled the country, and the Crown is now vested jointly in King William and Queen Mary."

Again he paused, watching the effect of his words. Bethany stared blankly back. The thing he had told them was too stupendous to be immediately absorbed. King James deposed, when only a few months ago the whole colony had been celebrating the birth of a Prince of Wales, a male heir to carry the Stuart dynasty on into the future? She stole a glance at Jared, and saw that he, too, was looking stunned.

"I have as yet," the Governor resumed, "received no commands concerning those who, like yourself, were sentenced to slavery for their part in Monmouth's rebellion, but it is plain that they can no longer be held guilty of treason against a monarch now deposed. Until such instruction comes, therefore, I am releasing you, Vernon, in the custody of Mr. Court, to whose service you were bound three years ago." His Excellency was still speaking gravely, but now there was a gleam of humor in his eyes. "How he deals with you is for him to decide. I am heartily glad to be rid of the problem."

Jared, for once at a loss, tried inadequately to express his gratitude, but this was cut firmly short. His Excellency invited them to take some refreshment before they returned to Courtlands, but excused himself from joining them on the score of much official business arising out of the news he had just received. He then summoned a servant to conduct them to another room, but added, as he took leave of them:

"One thing, Vernon, I will say. This colony has need of men such as you, trained soldiers of courage and resource. You came to Barbados as a convict slave; it is my hope that you will stay here, of your own free will, once your servitude is at an end."

To Bethany, the Governor's words were simply another marvel, part and parcel of this incredible hour. She still felt dazed, unable to grasp the enormity of what had happened; the transition from utter despair had been too swift, too complete, to be as yet wholly believable. She distrusted it, as though it were a bright bubble likely to vanish if she clutched at it too greedily.

The servant led them to another room, and poured wine and proffered sweetmeats, and she accepted both as though in a dream. Her father and Jared were silent, too. Like Bethany, they found it difficult to grasp the full significance of what had happened. Mr. Court was the first to speak.

"I think we should do well to be on our way," he said practically, setting down his glass. "The whole town will be buzzing like a bee-hive as soon as the news becomes known, and Vernon's release is likely to cause such jubilation that I would prefer to have Bethany safely at Courtlands before word of it is spread."

"A moment, sir!" Jared said quietly. "His Excellency is glad to be rid of the problem of my future, but I doubt whether you are equally pleased to have it thrust upon you. It is a devilish situation, and that's the truth!"

"I do not find it so," Mr. Court replied mildly. "You are released in my custody, but you need not fear that such authority will weigh too heavily upon you. Are you supposing me so lost to all sense of gratitude that I would send you back to the stockade?"

"I do not think it, sir, but that was not what I meant." Jared moved to where Bethany sat and took her hand, looking at Matthew Court with a distinct challenge in his eyes. "I have made no secret of my love for your daughter. I am bond to you now, but when I regain my freedom I shall marry her."

"Whether I give my consent or not," Mr. Court concluded for him as he paused. "Is it honesty, I wonder, or mere folly, to tell me that? You are well aware that it is for me to say whom my daughter shall wed, while you, as you remind me, are still my bond-servant. Thus I hold complete authority over you both." He looked from Jared's challenging gray eyes to Bethany's beseeching blue ones, and smiled. "To remove from you any temptation to defy that

uthority, I intend to bestow you upon each other
ith as little delay as possible."

Bethany gave a gasp of relief and joy, and
tretched out her free hand to her father, who took it
n both his own. A sudden light had leapt into Jared's
yes, and his voice was not quite steady as he said:
"Is that possible, sir?"

"I do not see why not. The Law gives a man
omplete authority over his slaves. I know of nothing
n it which forbids him to make one of them his
on-in-law, if he so chooses. Now, let us begone. I will
rrange for you to borrow a mount from the
overnor's stables." He laid his hand briefly on the
ounger man's shoulders. "I echo His Excellency, my
oy! It is my hope, too, that you will stay in Barbados.
ourtlands will have need of a new master one day."

He went out. Jared and Bethany looked won-
eringly at each other, still half afraid to believe in
his change in their fortunes, in the sudden lifting of
he shadow of parting and death. Her hand still
ested in his, and now she laid the other over it.

"Could you bear to stay here, Jared? I will go
nywhere in the world with you, but if you could...!"

He drew her up out of the chair, and took her in his
rms. "This is your home, my love. I have never had
ne rightfully to call my own, and where you will be
appiest, that shall be home to me. Your father and
lis Excellency seem to think I may be of some service
the colony. Do I not owe something to Barbados,
r giving me the most precious gift of my life?"

"And your own father, Jared?" she said hesi-
antly. "Your hope of vengeance? You could go back
England, once you are free."

He shook his head. "I think I would no longer find
im there. You heard what His Excellency said.
King James and certain gentlemen closest to him in
is counsels." St. Orme is bound to have been one of
hose who fled into exile, but even if he were not, I find

I do not hate him as I did." He drew her closer, looking down into her eyes. "You have my whole heart, Bethany. There is no room in it for anything but you." He kissed her, gently and very tenderly, for happiness was still too new and fragile to be roughly used. "Come, love! Let us go home."